NEW DIRECTIONS 41

New Directions in Prose and Poetry 41

Edited by J. Laughlin

with Peter Glassgold and Frederick R. Martin

 A New Directions Book

ACKNOWLEDGMENTS
Grateful acknowledgment is made to the editors and publishers of magazines in which some of the selections in this volume first appeared: for Samuel Hazo, *The Ontario Review* (Copyright © 1978 by Samuel Hazo) and *Tar River Poetry Review* (Copyright © 1979 by Samuel Hazo).

Montri Umavijani's "By the Clemency of Hell" and "Sketches for Purgatory" were originally printed, in 1977 and 1979 respectively, at the Prachandra Press, Maharaja Road, Bangkok, Thailand.

Due to an unfortunate error, the "Selected Poems of Patience Worth," edited by Stephen E. Braude and included in *New Directions in Prose and Poetry 40*, were incorrectly attributed to an "eighteenth-century personality." Patience Worth ought to have been called a "seventeenth-century personality." The editors of the anthology series regret any confusion their slip may have caused.—Eds.

Manufactured in the United States of America
First published clothbound (ISBN: 0–8112–0770–6) and as New Directions Paperbook 505 (ISBN: 0–8112–0771–4) in 1980
Published simultaneously in Canada by George J. McLeod, Ltd., Toronto

New Directions Books are published for James Laughlin
by New Directions Publishing Corporation,
80 Eighth Avenue, New York 10011

CONTENTS

THE TOO LATE AMERICAN BOYHOOD BLUES

FREDERICK BUSCH

Her father was a corresponding member of the Book-of-the-Month-Club, and I was a pale, stale college poet who wrote the Ginsberg pastiche and wore black. I was a virgin, and I was scared, and she was not. On the floor of her parents' living room, I defended a dream of virtue and the actual fact of my fright by withholding, by denying, by offering up a maiden's prayer. "Not until we're married," I whispered to Elaine, whom I would know for eleven months, as I looked up at the walls while we loved with our hands, grim little master mechanics, under gold-framed pictures her father had cut from magazines. I remember *The Rape of the Sabine Women*, whose rolling eyes justified the sacrifice of sexual pleasure, and there was *Galsworthy at the Heights in Highgate Cemetery*, a sad tall man in loose clothing who stood on a promontory of the north London graveyard to stare at the stones.

That was what I thought of as I signed the short-term lease for the flat—where else?—in Highgate, on the edge of Hampstead Heath. I was twice the age I'd been when I first heard of the cemetery, and I was there to spend a large foundation's funds in learning about Victorian crypts and sculpted headstones. Before I was settled in the flat, I had forgotten to think about early middle age, about a girl who had fully populated my seventeenth year, about another woman in America who had peopled my thirty-second, and thirty-third, and thirty-fourth, and then had changed

1

her ways, and mine, by settling in another man's life for what she described as the rest of her own. I had almost forgotten.

I thought instead about my budget, and TV rental, and reader's tickets at the British Museum and the V & A, about coming home through the Heath from Flask Walk in Hampstead, full of beer after closing time, and about how little I wanted to do my project and what a sizable amount of good I might derive from caring for my work. I gave myself a week for orientation, and then another week. I slept late, began receiving mail, said hello to Bert, the porter of the apartment building, said good-by in the morning to Toni, Bert's small wife, who washed down the hallways and scrubbed at the stoop. I rode on the Thames to see the *Cutty Sark*, ate in trattorias on Greek Street, walked one night from Covent Garden to Swiss Cottage before riding the last bus home.

Home was the narrow flat with flimsy imitation Danish furniture and a small kitchen smelling of enamel paint, a corridor opening into bedrooms, and me walking back and forth on the toes of my new Clark's desert boots, wondering what to do with this new life— all that money in the bank, all that good work waiting, all those letters from all those American friends, and all the time I owned because a woman I would live away from now was six hours earlier in her life than I was in mine.

I left a pub in Hampstead one evening at dusk, happy with whisky but sad about going home. So I walked on Hampstead Heath, where children in the pale lavendar light threw frisbees and kicked black-and-white soccer balls to their parents. I watched the young mothers as they ran to chase the balls. Their breasts moved contrapuntally to the happy pumping of their legs.

I went home, and I saw Bert, the porter, standing at the short brick pillar where the apartment block's name was posted. He wore a hard twill suit and highly polished black shoes. His hands were clasped behind his back, as if he mounted watch, and in the street-lights his glasses glimmered, his hard face looked red. "Hallo, Jeremy," he crowed, "you're looking a little seedy tonight."

"Evening, Bert. Nice to see you."

I walked past, but Bert's hand held my arm. The hand was strong, its grip failed to differentiate between me and, say, the handle of a wrench or rake. "Jeremy, I'm happy to see you. On my word now, word of honor, I've had a few pots at the boozer. I went to see the police surgeon's people—did you know I was a copper twenty years? Not a bent minute, I swear to God. It was my stomach retired me." Bert's face rippled and a pain ran down it toward his gut, which he rubbed. He held my arm.

I had held arms too hard, and I decided that the next morning I would walk up to the cemetery and start to work. I said, as if I cared, "Bert, you all right? Everything all right?"

He dropped his hand, adjusted his stance to his drunk wobble, and said with too much matter-of-fact denials, "No, it isn't anything, Jeremy, I suppose. They don't actually *know*, in point of fact. It's these stomach tests they've been giving me."

"Bisodol," I said. "No: barium."

"That's it. They make you swallow it. You see, they don't know what I've got." Leaning in, gripping my arm again, speaking in a hoarse and confidential voice, he said, "They want to cut me open, don't they?"

"What does that mean, Bert? I mean, how bad is that?"

"Listen!" he said, falling back a few inches against the pillar. "Now, I've had a few pints, but I am not drunk. I swear to God, and you must promise me, word of honor, not to say a word to Toni. I'd not like her to know."

I said the sounds I could think of to say, including "Don't worry" and "Everything yet" and "Hardly cause for" and the coveted "Good night," and I was in my foyer, turning the lock, switching on the television set, heating the kitchen grill, staying inside for the night as far as I could get.

I walked up to Highgate Cemetery next morning. The high iron gates beside the abandoned charnel house, which looked like medieval ruins, were locked. Inside the gates, standing near a small stone shed, an old man in a loud sport jacket and dark dirty pants hushed the small white dog that raged at me. I passed through the bars a letter from the president of the Hampstead and Highgate Historical Society, and the dog took it, shook it, and dropped it onto the mud and gravel. "Jeremy Selden," I shouted through the bars.

"Who's he?" the man called over his dog's reply.

"Me."

"What's the letter about, then?"

"Getting into the cemetery."

"It's closed."

"He said you'd open it for me."

"Who? Seldom?"

"No, I'm Seldom. I'm *Selden*."

"You wrote the letter?"

"No. Look, I don't remember his name, but he's the man who wrote the letter your dog was eating."

"And he said you could come in?"

"He said he'd talk to you."

"Nobody talked to *me*."

"Would you read the letter?"

"Oh, gladly."

The dog barked, the man read, we discussed my name, and then he said something to the dog, perhaps correcting *his* pronunciation of my name, and the dog stopped barking, and while I was led to a wide rutted avenue of mud and stones, the dog went into the shed. "Been closed forever," he told me. "And they can't afford to keep it up. That one"—a stone sarcophagus with an eight-inch-thick stone lid split down the middle—"it got hit by one of the V-bombs during the war and there it is. They'll never repair it. That one"—another sarcophagus lid, this one shoved aside by a slender tree—"the Australians sent us a gift of ash trees. Grew like Kaffirs, and no one to maintain 'em. Now they're taking over. The days here are numbered, I'm afraid."

Stones leaned, many were down, most were defaced by painted and sprayed initials and important youthful decisions: WOGS OUT and RANGERS RULE OK. The grass was high and yellow, the small tough ash trees were crowding out the older growth, and shiny green leaves reflected the light metallically, so that their brilliance, and the crowding ash trees, made a sense of jungled darkness behind the stones. He showed me where Galsworthy had sat to look at graves. We walked up a muddy hill, into dense growth, to see the stones of Charles Dickens's parents. We walked down the slope around a curve, down cracked and mossy steps, into a small street that was bordered on both sides by what seemed to be broken walls. Then I saw that they were crypts, many of them opened, all of them defaced. NIGS OUT. The tombs gave off a coldness and they blocked the light, and it was time to leave.

At his shed, he gave me a map and told me when I might come

to do my work. He called me "Professor Seldom," and I tried to give him fifty pence. "Nice to know someone takes it seriously," he said as he refused. I felt like raising him to a pound because I almost didn't care, but instead I shook his hand—the white dog shifted and made a throat-noise—and then I went past the charnel house, home. And because the necessary arrangements were made, and I could start in next morning to do some serious early work at the cemetery, I naturally got up late instead and rode the bus to West Kensington and the V & A. We passed Harrod's, where I had shopped once on a trip with the woman who no longer cared to live with me, and I got off at the next stop, walked back down the street, and browsed in the Harrod's food halls, paying a good deal of attention to goods I wouldn't buy. I sneered at some fellow Americans, purchased a bottle of extremely good unblended malt whisky, then went upstairs to the book department where I bought a new Desmond Bagley, thought twice about the budget, took a taxi all the way back to Highgate, and stayed inside, drinking somewhat too much, watching a documentary on Midlands potteries. I tried to keep my toilet from running.

The flushbox mounted on the wall kept filling too full, and the overflow pipe that led through the outside wall to the ground near the stoop kept running. I called Bert, and he arrived later to inspect. He told me that a Russian-born Jewish novelist who lived upstairs had been making complaints about the spillage. I said I'd never read her. "Oh, no one hereabouts reads her," Bert said, "but she's very famous in the district nevertheless. Quite rich off the sales of her books, I'm told. Now, she's one of the reasons you may see me walking about of an evening with a spanner in one hand and a flashlight in the other. It's no emergency, and you needn't fear. But the building, you see, is fairly jumping with Jews. And London, even up here, has gone down to the dogs. With the Arabs buying the big house up at the top of Highgate West Hill Road, well, you never know, do you, who's planting explosives someplace. I'm to see they don't do it here. I was a copper once, remember."

I thought of the embattled Russian novelist, coping with fame and wealth and the P.L.O., and I did go back up the hill to the cemetery next morning. The old man showed me its other side, across the road, where Marx was buried. We discussed communism, labor unions, Arab oil embargoes, and the price of real estate. He left me to work, and I didn't. I wandered among the stones, reading names I didn't know, looking out of the fence at the mothers pushing prams and the patrons leaving the public library across the street. I wondered if any of them carried a book by a Russian-Jewish lady whose perimeters were patrolled each night by a metastisizing former cop.

And that night, Bert was there to clatter tools and unscrew nuts in the bathroom, clear his throat and grunt with his efforts. I stayed in the little living room and finished the Bagley thriller. When Bert was done, we stood together to watch the toilet triumphantly flush. I offered him two pounds. His eyes stayed fuzzy behind his strong glasses, but his face tightened, and he waved a hand. "No thanks," he said. "I was twenty years a copper and I never took tuppence. No thanks."

"But I'm not a crook," I said, wondering if the foundation would agree. "I wanted to thank you. No insult intended."

"None taken, my word of honor. No money either, though." Bert hung on the toilet chain again, and again it stammered and roared. Then he rubbed his hands together and smiled, said, "Even with villains though, and surely you aren't one, though not a fountain of information about yourself either, I have been known to take a friendly drink."

So in the small sitting room with its aquamarine carpet and the half-glued furniture of a third-class hotel, we sipped malt whisky and Bert talked about English crooks and early retirement and the malefactors to be found near the Billingsgate fish markets, hard by Guy's Hospital, where there still stands a bar at which doctors drank with grave robbers who sold cadavers for medical students. He and Toni were Welsh, he said, "Which explains why that woman's so hard." He sat with his legs tightly crossed, elbows in his lap, chin down. Sometimes, as if he twisted his face to find a word, pain made a pattern on his lips, and they seemed to slowly flutter. There was goose flesh on his arms in the overheated room. I looked, and made assumptions, and insisted to myself that I was young and working at my job and that solitude was rarely sickness.

"Oh, she's a proper bitch, that woman, you make *no* mistake," Bert said. He sipped and shuddered, clamped his legs upon himself, pushed his glasses back onto the bridge of his nose. "Jeremy—we're friends, I think. I swear to God, Jeremy, but she's tough. The youngest in a family of eight. What did you say your line of work was?"

I mentioned the history of Victorian art, then asked some questions about Wales, then screwed the cap back onto the whisky. "Good old Jeremy," Bert said to the room. "He knows how to tell you to piss off without hurting your feelings all that badly. I beg your pardon. But I have had a drink."

It was the sheerest romanticism, and the people under those stones might have loved it: Jeremy Selden, dismal in his life, sitting over gravemeat and bones, writing notes about the decorations of the dead. But I worked there that next morning, and felt that I was coming to the point where I might start to really do some honest labor. So I rewarded myself by riding to the piers where I caught the boat to Kew Gardens. It was too early for the full display of tulips, but there was a lot of red and yellow to look at, and the fine arching glass building—someone under Highgate Cemetery had designed it, I was sure—in which breadfruit bloomed and tropical mists rode the circular iron ladder to the high gallery. That night, I saw Alec Guinness on TV, a ship's captain who cavorted under similar trees on a mythical island, and I smiled because we were colleagues.

And then in the morning, a scraping sound at the kitchen window—Toni, on the stone stoop, smearing suds and spattering gray water. Her face was sealed. And then, in the later morning, just after closing time, Bert was at the door. He smiled and offered half a pint of Haig. "I beg your pardon, Jeremy," he said, "but I have had a drink. I've made so bold as to buy us a bottle at the boozer in the hopes you'll have the kindness to join me." I cleared the kitchen table of its coffee cup and half-filled milk bottle. Seeing it, Bert grinned. "Stomach trouble?" he asked. "Ah, that's a killer, that one."

Trapped, I sipped small. Bert gulped, in the victory of entrapment. He crossed his legs, shuddered as the whisky dropped, then delivered a monologue about a crook he'd caught who was a painter. Bert had purchased one of his canvases "for the cloud formation." He said, "I'm a sketcher, did you know that? I'm an artist. I know something about clouds, and that yobbo was good. He was a leatherer, mind you, I don't mean to say he had much of a soul. He'd leather you from behind with a great cosh and kill you, if it happened that way, so he could lift your wallet and that would be that. But he was a lad with some talent. I thought you'd like knowing that, you being a student of the arts and all."

I poured more whisky for him, sipped at my own glass, nodded. Bert shuddered, flicked his cigarette ash onto the floor, and seemed to wind his legs tighter as he smiled and then grimaced—the lips worked from one expression into the other with no interruption: his smile was of pain, his sign of suffering a pleasantry. He said, "Have you missed the cats?"

"What?"

"The big fuckin' howlers outside at the edge of the Heath, where the garden begins. Surely you've heard them, Jeremy. That big black fucker who screams like a little child?"

"No," I said. Then: "I heard that one, one night."

"How could you not?" Bert sipped, I poured more for each of us, and Bert made the face and hung his head, then sat up straighter, leaned forward, elbows on the table. "He was a particularly savage one, that bastard." Bert shook his head as if a small insect threatened his eye. "The tenants, you see, they're a proper lot of rich Jews. They've made their money. They don't like the smell of cat-pee on the garage walls. They don't like the sounds the brutes make. They don't *like*. And I'm out there on my Arab patrol, and you know what these people are? Yourself excepted, of course. They're a mob of fat, moneyed cowards." Spit popped onto Bert's lower lip and into the air. He shook his head again. "They couldn't do it themselves, don't you see. So they come cringing and whining to me, and I'll do it, I'll *do* it, all right, I'll kill the cats for 'em. You know how I killed the big black bastard with the little baby's cry at two in the morning when the Jews are asleep and the Arabs come out?"

He sat back in his chair and his chest swelled, his arm rose over his shoulders and his nose lifted as if he addressed a threat: "I took ahold of him. I had my spanner, you see." His face was white with rage, his lips were compressed and they disappeared into the whiteness of the face. "I took him, and I hit him and hit him and hit him and hit him"—the scrawny arm rising and falling, rising and shuddering down to the table top—"and I said all right, you bastard, come on, you bastard, let's go, you bastard yobbo son of a bitch bastard son of a bitch." The voice that came through clenched teeth was thick with mucus and fury, the square face shook on its slender corded neck.

He lifted his glass, put it down, lifted it with two hands and carefully drank. His breath hissed out, and he set his trembling hands in his lap, recrossing his legs. "I'm not necessarily a violent man," Bert said in a lower voice, almost hoarse. "I'm really not. But I was a tough copper. I know how to do the job. I swear to God. I've got cancer of the stomach, Jeremy. I had another verdict from the police surgeon's office. I beg your pardon. I'm a little boozed up. I've had a few drinks to drink. I am dying."

Bert's expression, muscular tension, even his smell—a compound of talcum, alcohol, tobacco, and old sweat—were unchanged. My back was suddenly wet, and perspiration tickled my sides. "They're sure?" I said.

Bert held up the arm which had just been killing cats, and he squeezed the broad forearm, much thicker than the pulpy-looking biceps, pulling at arteries that snaked just under the surface. "I'm losing weight, Jeremy. Look at this." He tore at the skin, as if to pluck it off. "Is this what a man looks like?"

"I had a friend who had polyps," I said, hating my voice.

"Cancer, Jeremy. I'm dying. They say they'd like to cut into me and have a look because there's supposed to be some small doubt about these famous tests of theirs."

"Do it, Bert. Try it."

"Once they cut you, Jeremy, you're dead. The trick now is not to let them in. Word of honor, I'm dying and you mustn't say a word to Toni."

"All right. Word of honor."

"I haven't told her, you see, and I don't want her to know. She's tough, she'll be all right, she'll be fine. Believe me. Your word of honor?"

"Word of honor."

"Because I think I can do it. I think I can live it through to my regular—the scheduled end." Bert laughed at the whisky he lifted toward his face. Then his face changed again, the tumbler struck the table top, and Bert was closer, then, to the black alley where he slaughtered cats: "I don't want her to *know*. I can live it out. But she mustn't be told."

"Word of honor," I said.

I had given that word before: to the woman with whom I had lived in recent years, to the State Department when I asked for passport renewal, to my banker when asking for loans, to the children of friends when I'd promised small certainties in their immediate future—gifts and snowfalls, the absence of ghosts—and withholding from a stranger's wife the manner of his dying seemed to me, alone in another country and a foreigner maybe to myself, only one more truth or one more lie to be told. I capped Bert's bottle and put it near his hand. Bert, always the diplomat, banged from chair to doorsill to foyer and out.

It rained the next morning, a gray, hard London spring rain, and I felt for the first time the excitement of what's alien, heard with pleasure the whine of the electric milk truck, smelled with hunger the English bacon in the doorway of the cafe across from the bus stop; harsh tobacco in the crowded bus made me want to smoke; the building's responsiveness to *other* demands for space and light made me smile as if in discovery. I read *The Guardian* through on my way to the V & A, and I noted with considerable pleasure that an advertisement was printed in Arabic, with English lettering condensed beneath the soft, rippled foreign words. It was good to see that occasional men in the streets, though they carried black umbrellas, wore long white robes and were followed by women in darker robes. Selden of Arabia.

The manuscripts I sought were in the Forster Collection, given to Dickens's friend and executor by Alec Hughes, a devotee of Dickens who had traveled widely in Ireland and Wales, collecting grave rubbings and interviewing the men—and one woman, who lived outside Galway—who had created tombs and headstones. The books, wide as business ledgers and bound in red leather, were brought to me on a gray, metal, rubber-wheeled cart. I found many examples of the usual inscription—"As you are now/So once was I," etc.—and sketches of funerary sculpture that were ancient-looking, little more than Celtic crosses; but there were angels suckling infants such as I had not seen, and accounts of greengrocers who buried people as a sideline, and one story of a man in Oughterard who had tried to embalm his wife according to what he swore was an original Egyptian recipe. And while I had a lot of information after a day's reading and scribbling and drinking coffee in the dark cafeteria, I was pleased to decide that I still had to travel to Ireland if the job were to be properly done. Moving, it struck me, was an art.

Walking down the steps of the museum, I wandered into a flock of schoolgirls in blue blazers and short plaid skirts; the nun who herded them blew a silver whistle and they stood still, giggling, until I was out of their midst. Down the street, a tall broad American—his tan raincoat was stiff and new as a flag—was pointing his finger at a short blonde woman in a stiff belted trenchcoat. Behind them was a broad man, shorter than the woman, wearing a burnoose and carrying a small red woman's umbrella that didn't prevent his powder-blue suit from turning dark with rain. The Arab wiped his mouth, with embarrassment I guessed, or annoyance, as the tall American pointed his finger again and gave the sort of order that I often saw businessmen in London give their wives. Though I usually had to guess, I was certain I was right: No, *you* make the reservations if we have to go to the goddamn theater tonight. Or: You want to go shopping? So go *shopping*, I came here to *work*. Or: I called him a fag because he's a fag. They're *all* fags here, aren't they?

What I wanted was what was different, what was away, the feeling of things as foreign to America as I felt then to me, and I stood too long with my briefcase full of monuments, I guess, or stared too hard with too much resentment. Because the woman felt me there. She looked up, squinted, reached into her bag for eyeglasses—his finger still hung in the air before her—and she called, in a voice I knew, "Selden? I don't believe this. Selden? Get your ass down here!"

It is true that you meet much of your past in foreign capitals; a life isn't so unpopulated or escapable, I guess, as you might like to think. That banality is acceptable. If it *is* a small world, then I'm prepared to make accommodations, and to work a little harder at sidling into its corners. But—Highgate Cemetery, Book-of-the-Month-Club, coitus deferred, and living room carpet—some coincidences are intolerable, and not so much because they occur but because of their particularity. To meet your dentist in New Orleans —all right; to trip in a Provençal restaurant on the handbag of the only transvestite you met in New Hope, Pennsylvania—perhaps; but to stagger into business such as ours, so unfinished: that is to admit of *certainties* in a life. Because so much of my life was uncertain, then, and had to be dealt with as a slowly developing emergency, minute to minute, and *not* in response to a past that dictated terms, I flapped my briefcase against my leg and I walked through the schoolgirls. The silver whistle blew again, and again they giggled and drifted in place, and she called, "Selden! Hey: it's me."

Her footsteps made me slow my pace, her voice made me stop, blushing. The tall American and short Arab walked slowly after her, and I watched them, then looked down to see the oval face and slightly cleft chin, the long nose, blonde hair. Her voice: wind over reeds I had called it in twelve or thirteen awful poems, and I had, though awful, been right. There was a breathiness to any word she said that made the hearer want that word to mean far more than it could have. In the dark especially, her voice had been charged with sex, even if it said that the fuses were blown.

She was saying, "Are you still a poet?" when the men arrived, and we all stood in the rain for introductions. Barney Korn, her husband. Mister Halabi, her husband's business associate. Jeremy Selden, an old friend. Mister Halabi put on blue-tinted glasses and made some gestures across his chest. Barney Korn nodded and didn't shake hands. I shrugged my shoulders and told them hello. And though it still should not have been happening, I wanted to say to her, "I have been with women, and not always unsatisfactorily. I only was scared. Though you were a kid, I was more of one. I'm a *late bloomer*, Elaine." We made perfunctory passes at mentioning import-export trading and the scholarship that always seems trivial compared to moving masses of tomato paste or wool across borders, and we stopped a cab and asked the driver to cross against traffic to take us to Harrod's for tea. I wanted to say, "You go to Fortnum and Mason's for tea," but I only smiled and sat curled on the jump seat to sneak looks at her legs while Mister Halabi made uneasy faces and Barney Korn asked her, as if I weren't there, "Where did you know him from?"

He decided, before she answered, that we didn't want tea, did we, so Korn directed the driver to take us down the street to a pub he had heard of named The Bunch of Grapes. Whoever read *Gourmet* in the States had heard of it too, and most of the subscribers were there. Korn complained about warm beer and ordered Scotch on ice. Elaine ordered brandy and I did too. Mister Halabi ordered Vermouth and drank it quickly, as if to sneak it down before I noticed that this Arab gentleman had swerved from dietary law. Barney Korn, leaning over the little table, said, "Mister Halabi is a Christian Jordanian." Mister Halabi smiled—it was the sort of smile that Bert might offer over drinks—and he cleaned his blue glasses by rubbing them against his wet suit coat; they smeared, but he put them on. Elaine asked questions—was I married, was I divorced, where did I work, what kind of museum was that, and how long would I be in London, and did I know it well, and why didn't I show her around while Barney and Mister Halabi conducted business?

Barney Korn was not only very tall, he was broad-shouldered and tough-looking. His hands were wide and short-fingered, his arms looked thick even in a business suit. His face, though smooth-shaven, looked rough with irritations. His nose had been broken once, and it was small and crooked. His hair was curly and tight. He made himself swell as he looked me over and nodded his agreement to Elaine's suggestion. He said again, "Where did you know each other?"

"In college," Elaine said.

"This guy—" He looked at me, then said, "You went to Vassar too?"

"No, when *I* was in college. Lafayette," I said. "Your wife was in high school."

"Couple of eager beavers," Korn said.

"What is that, please?" Mister Halabi asked softly.

"Hey," Korn said, "you know what?" He smiled, and the coarseness of his skin smoothed out somehow, the nose looked only charming, not tough. He spoke in the lowest of voices all the time, and that was the realest threat—you had to bend to hear him, and he surely knew that: he wanted you to obey. I thought of the nun's whistle and how innocent its shrillness was, compared to the murmur of the man who made you bend.

"Those are animals, are they not?" Mister Halabi asked.

"Listen," Korn said, as casually as if he offered a cigarette. He did, and Halabi, shrugging, took one. "I think I'm jealous, Jerry."

"Jeremy," she told him.

"Jeremy. I think I am. You know? It's peculiar that you knew my wife before I did."

"Somewhat like the English badger, I believe," Mister Halabi said.

"Why don't we *all* see the sights together, then?" I said.

Mister Halabi was looking, and listening, and drinking his second vermouth. What I said knocked his glass to the table and his shoulders back against the chair. His neck moved forward, and he said, "Ah, business first, I fear, Mister Selden. We are a people of business, you know. Have you noticed that London has changed? She is a trading city, now that we are here. You know this? We are traders." He whispered too, lower than Korn. I had no idea about his accent, and I had no sense of the Arab peoples either, except that they owned all the oil, and much of London, and were said to want to kill the Jews. Mister Halabi smiled and said, "It is our way."

"Business," Korn said. "You two guys, go ahead. Get me some souvenirs for the girls in the office. She can tell be about it. Jerry—Jeremy, excuse me. You want to tell me about your research?"

"Not a lot," I said. "You want to hear about it?"

"Not really," he said, smiling that good smile. "Let's get going, okay? You two meet each other someplace tomorrow, how's that?"

Elaine said, "You decide for us, Selden."

"A ride on the Thames. That's where to start. Then from the piers we go into the City. It's the original city of London."

"The banks are there," Halabi said.

"And then we see," I said.

"Hey," Korn said, wagging his thick finger at me as he'd shaken it earlier at her, "you guys watch that then-we-see stuff, huh?" He smiled his smile, his low voice disappeared, and then the smile did, but not because he hadn't meant it, I think, so much as because he and Mister Halabi were moving, and then so was Elaine, and not without some pleasure taken by them all in the stern pace. I wondered if I ought to live in America anymore, and then I wondered where else I should live. I said to her, "Westminster Piers, you can take the underground."

"A cab," Korn said, buttoning his raincoat. "She'll be there at nine, ten o'clock, right? She'll take a cab."

Elaine turned to say, "I still don't believe it. We're here on business and what do we find? Unfinished business. And it's how old?"

"Never mind," Korn pretended to growl. He smiled again, waved his hand at me, and walked. Mister Halabi made nervous gestures on the front of his suitcoat and followed.

Elaine bent toward the table and said, "Never *mind* never mind. You be there, Selden."

"I will," I said. "I will. Word of honor."

Which was what Bert heard from me, again, that night, when we sat in my kitchen under a blue-gray cloud of his smoke, surrounded by my late dinner he had come to watch me finish while he drank the navy rum he'd brought. "This is true, Jeremy," he said, signaling that, after meandering through names of pubs and words which crooks and doctors had spoken, he at last had arrived at the right address. "I'll tell you something. It's an interesting study in psychology. I haven't had sex with my wife for—yes, it's five years. Toni? My wife?"

Even to a man such as I, who had little ease with people at their best, much less in the darkness of their intimacies, this was familiar terrain. Everyone has been there before. There no longer are words to be spoken in reply because this is the place of blackness in somebody's life. These are the sounds someone makes instead of killing animals at night.

"You've seen how smooth her face is? How tight her bust—Jesus God, her breasts stand straight up! That cost me nearly two thousand pounds over the years, and on a copper's pay this is, and with no money taken on the side, I swear to God. Two thousand sodding quid. If you look very close next time you see her, you can find the little white lines around the ears. That would be your tip-off. She's had her breasts made smaller and her face tightened up. It sounds like repairing some fucking *car,* doesn't it? She's fifty-two, and now she thinks she looks twenty-two, and for her it's like when she was in the WAAF at the end of the war. That's what she wanted, you see. She wanted everything the way it was.

"And you know who had to change the dressings? You know who had to peel those bandages off with their runny pus and put the fresh dressings on? You're looking at him. Of course. I do the dirty work around here, don't I? You just think of the cats you don't hear. Now, I did try to go to bed with her. I swear to God. It's important in this to be fair. I did try. I'd get into bed, after she was healed, and I'd put my hand on her breast, and I'd feel stitches. I'd feel these soft little rubbery bumps. Scars. I thought I would vomit onto her first time I tried it. Jesus God. Stitches, all the scars even after she'd healed. You see? Can you imagine it? I was going to bed with Frankenstein. I was touching Frankenstein, and her all moving about on the bed and thinking she was beautiful, you see, that's the part I hated as much as any other."

When Bert stopped and drank and poured more, lit a new ciga-
rette, looked into me for response, I knew that nothing should be
said because nothing would be heard. Bert was talking to me from
the place where there really weren't words. "I'm an artist," he said,
"a sketcher. If I made a sketch of her, the way she really looks, she
couldn't stand it, could she? She wants to look the way she looked
in 1948. But I'm an artist. I make things look the way things are.
It's the only way a cop could see things. She couldn't stand it. My
word of honor. Do you know a woman with five mirrors in her
bedroom? No, thank you. I'll stay on the booze, thank you. And
she can sleep alone. She's got what she wants, she's a tough little
bitch, and she's welcome to it all. *I* don't know her. *I* don't know
who she is. And that is why, now you have to listen to me: that is
exactly why you're not to say a word about this thing to her. My
little time bomb. You've promised me, remember. Your word of
honor."

"Word of honor," I said.

I moved the rum bottle closer to Bert, but he dropped his ciga-
rette onto the floor and stood, managed eventually to step on the
butt, staggering. He said with great dignity, "Well, I'm off, then.
You'll have to come and have a meal with us, Jeremy. You'll do
that, I hope." He slowly turned, pulled the kitchen cupboard open,
and walked into cooking oil and cornflakes. I took him to his flat
with one hand tightly clamped around his biceps, letting him lean
his little weight against me. To watching tenants, Russian novelists,
I must have looked like a friendly policeman helping the neighbor-
hood drunk along his way.

That night, I drank some of the rum Bert had left, and I wrote a
letter to the woman who had recently left me. I wrote four letters
to her. Addressed to the New York apartment she no longer kept,
they all began with a chipper *Hey, here I am in London,* and then,
like our discussions of marriage, our later talks about growing old
in different places, our final conversations on the subject of know-
ing each other at all, the letters fell into staccato statements about
need. My last letter said, *You didn't need me. You were right. And
I am exquisitely tired of needing you.* "If it's just need," she had
said, "you could raise some tropical fish. They'd count on you." I
was hardly drunk, and surely far from drunk enough to write three
thousand miles, and six hours, about necessity, when what really

appalled me was how ill at ease I had grown with Jeremy Selden. He would have to apply for a passport to live even with me, I decided. I carried the letters to the toilet and burned them above the bowl. Jeremy, the Druid, makes sacrifices. I pulled the chain and flushed them down. As I turned the TV set on to watch a Cockney detective, I hoped that Bert's repairs had been inadequate, and that the Russian novelist would slip on spilled-over water and crack a small bone on the leaked solutions of a lover lost in London. "Tolstoy of Arabia," I told the guy with the gun.

I wore a tweed sport coat over a sweater and therefore was dressed in too little for a chilly day; the idea was to look like an Englishman, so many of whom dressed as if the world were always fifty-five degrees. The idea, of course, was to leave my own tan raincoat home because I knew that Elaine would wear hers. She did, and she was warm on the deck of the *Queen Boadicea* as we cut away from the pier near the Houses of Parliament and sailed. Mist lay over the river, and I wanted to tell her that underneath it, rolling in the strong current, were drowned three-legged dogs and sacks of garbage and, beneath them, according to the Greater London Council, salmon good for eating and, lower still, phosphorescent with rot, the bodies of the dead. I pointed out handsome buildings by Christopher Wren, and then the pilot told us on his loudspeaker that we were passing Lime House, where the pirates once were hung in chains to be drowned by the tides. He told us everything else, and she stopped listening and so did I. Like kids, we held hands. Like kids, we watched each other from secret places and waited to be caught. When we got off and were sitting on the bus going back to the City, we weren't talking about London or villains in their chains, but about her life with Barney Korn, the car he had offered on her thirty-first birthday, the death of her father, her mother's happy widowhood.

"Don't take this wrong," I said, "but I bet he died of stomach cancer."

"Why?"

"Did he?"

"Heart. A heart attack."

"That's a relief, believe it or not."

"*Why?*"

"The story is just ridiculous, believe me, pal."

"You always called me kitten," she said. "It made you feel older than me."

"I *was* older than you. I still am."

"No," she said. "I always was older than you. We're maybe the same age now." And, as ever, I delighted in the sound of her voice; she could have been telling me the weather, instead of the truth.

Barney was rich, he was older than she was and older than I, and she thought he did some peculiar forms of business. "So why do you stay with him? If he's a crook."

"I don't know if he's a crook. He's my husband. He is wonderful in bed, Selden. You'd never know it, but he is absolutely insane, he's a genius at it. And he completely loves me."

"Is this the part where I ask if you love him?"

"Only if you're nasty."

Barney was on the board of a synagogue in Syosset, where they kept their magical bed and parked the cars he gave her, and Barney's great regret, she told me, was that they had no children he might raise—males, of course—to lead the community, or state, or world.

"Yeah," I said, "I was wondering about that. He's such a heartfelt Jew, how come he traffics with Arab mercenaries?"

"Kantibhai Patell?"

"Who?"

"Halabi. Don't you know anything about foreign people, Selden? Barney is a bigot just like everyone else. Hates the Arabs. Hates Brown's, where I made him get us rooms. Half of the suites were taken by Arabs. He can't *stand* them. They're going to burn our mattress, he thinks."

"Whereas you and he are doing that all on your own."

"Easy. I'm sorry I told you that. I wanted you to get excited. No, he really *does*—but he figured, you're in London doing business these days, you better hang around with an Arab. You look like you have a lot of backing, you know? So he hired Kantibhai Patell, he works for Barney's bank here. He turned Kantibhai Patell into Halabi from Jordan. You *believe* it?"

"Barney is very creative," I said. Then I added, "As you've made clear."

Near St. Paul's, we entered the narrow door of the City Vaults, then walked down two flights to its huge, high stone-walled cellar, where businessmen stood at the bar to drink wine, and couples sat at round tables to eat roast beef and ham. We sat too, and drank half a bottle of the house claret before the meal came, then finished the bottle and drank most of another. I ordered port for us, and while we waited for the waitress to bring us each a second glass, we finished the second bottle of wine. And by then, we were admitting how we used to walk across the Parade Grounds near Fort Hamilton Parkway in Brooklyn, kissing a lot on the way, and how we used to go to the movies, where I would sit with my arm around her, my hand under her sweater, after she had opened her brassière catch, and how, on the floor of her parents' apartment, we would writhe and gasp and speak our love and ejaculate our love and never *make* our love.

"You were so scared," she said, leaning at the wine bottle, then leaning back as the port came. "You know what I figured? You were chubby. I figured you were embarrassed to show your tush. I didn't want to say that in those days. I mean, I did, but I was afraid to. I wanted to tell you I liked your ass, and anyway we could have done it with your pants on."

I shifted and said, as calmly as I could, "You know, I never thought of that."

"Sure you did. You thought of everything."

"I kept thinking I was scared."

"Oh, well you were. You were. I was too, but *I* was scared because I was such an easy lay."

"So you were glad we—didn't."

"I think so. Yes. But I also really wanted to. You're blushing."

Which made me blush more, and which made me order more port. If I could have, I would have started a small fire to divert her attention ,and mine. Thinking about fire made me think about their mattress in Syosset, and the one at Brown's, and I said, in what must have been the voice I used at seventeen in that apartment— choked with humiliation at the distance between who I was and who I wanted me to be—"Better late than never, maybe. Do you think?"

"Oh," she said, "Selden, you *had* to be thinking that back at the museum."

"Well," I said. "Were you?"

"Didn't you hear what I said to you? Get your *ass* down here, I said. I was thinking of your teen-age tush."

So it was required that I leave some money on the table, that we walk up the stairs, that we find a taxi and persuade the driver to ride all the way to Highgate.

In the cab, near Kentish Town, I said, "Does Barney follow you around?"

"You mean suspicious-husband following?"

"Or his hired hand. Because an Arab guy was on the street where we got the cab, and he got into one behind us. Look."

"Selden, how many black taxis are there in London?"

"With Arabs in them?"

"Even with Arabs. They probably bought the cabs."

"Yeah."

"He trusts me."

"Why?"

She leaned over and kissed me under the ear, and I remembered—I smelled it, then—Old Spice after shave lotion, which I always used to put there because she liked it. I remembered Johnny Mathis records on the stereo set in the apartment, and a song about getting misty when someone thought of someone else—presumably, in those days, me.

But I looked back, we were on the outskirts of Highgate, and I saw the cab, with perhaps a foreign headress floating in the back, and I said to the driver, "Highgate Cemetery, please. Main gate."

"You're still showing me the sights?"

"If anyone asks."

The gates were locked. The dog was there, but not his master, so we walked along the black, high iron fence, and I pointed to slanting stones in the yellow grass. Her only response was, "How far do you live from here?"

"Would you like to see where Marx is buried?"

"I'd rather see where Selden's buried."

"Oh, Jesus, Elaine."

"Big baby."

"Yes. It's just down the road."

Bert wasn't outside, neither was Toni, though I was certain that Mrs. Tolstoy was watching us and making notes. Elaine walked through the flat, told me I was a good housekeeper, went back up the hall to the bedroom I was using, and closed the café curtains. In the half-darkness of the room, she took her raincoat off, and her shoes, and then the tan silk blouse and brown tweed skirt. Her brassière was blue, and so were her panties. So, in fact, were my boxer shorts, which she discovered when she loosened my belt and pulled my trousers down.

She sat in front of my feet, with her knees drawn up, her toes touching my heaped pants. "You seem to have a perfectly sweet behind, Selden. It's nice to meet it after all these years." She pulled at the shorts, they went down, and she turned me by grasping my knees. When my back was to her, she rose and moved her lips up the back of my right leg until their warmth and little nibbles reached the buttock, where she nibbled harder, bit, then kissed me. I turned, we bumped all over, took the rest of her clothes off, and mine, and in the chilly room, in the artificial darkness of rooms where love is made in the daytime—it is the most faraway place, such a room; it can make for shivering with make-believe and the mysteries of travel—we resumed the unfinished business.

Except that I stopped. "*Did* you see anyone on the street behind us?" I begged.

She pulled my face down to her breasts again.

"You're a married woman, Elaine."

"I'm your teen-age girlfriend."

"I'm—"

Holding my face there, then pulling my hair, and very hard, she whispered, "You better not, Selden."

"No," I said. "Except there is an Arab assassin stalking us, who is of course an Indian bank clerk named Kantibhai Patell. And a husband who sent him after us who is four inches taller than me and probably a Golden Gloves champion, or maybe an all-Ivy tackle. And the fact that we are . . . what we're doing—"

She twisted my hair. "Selden, don't you start in playing those too-late-all-American-boyhood-blues at me."

I nuzzled into her. I moaned, "I love this."

"You better."

"I love you."

"You better *not*." And then she twisted too hard, and I bit her, and she clubbed me on the side of the head, and pulled at me, and I pushed, and we conducted unfinished business. The initial conference was a short one. So then we discussed, in some detail, the conduct of business in the past. Our appetites became whetted for more work, and we went back to it while the day outside lay hard and silver on the fibrous curtains, and there were motions, seconds, immediate action, delaying action, gestures of great generosity, instants of understandable profit-taking, and because one of us specialized in research there was deep delving, scrupulous examination, hard study, and joy in the results. We did celebrate free enterprise and, simultaneously, man's thirst for knowledge. We consummated deals.

I wanted to say, "I did need this," and I think I did. Because she said, "Me too." I wanted to ask her why, since Barney was the marvel of the industry. But I didn't. I thought to say, "I need you." But I didn't.

And she must have known. For as we pulled the blankets up, she said, "Remember, Selden. We aren't seventeen, either of us. That's the only time you're allowed to pretend you can have what you want."

"I feel like I'm seventeen."

"Sure. But you only get that once."

"So I'm seventeen and thirty-four at the same time."

"Only for now. It goes away."

"Yeah. And you go away."

"I'll write you," she whispered. Her skin was warm, and it was so smooth that I didn't want to stop stroking it. "No more now," she said. "Sleep. Stop thinking." Then: "You never knew how to do that, did you?"

It was Halabi who woke me, from the small garden walk behind the bedroom windows, against the curtains of which the light was gold when I sat up. I mean, it was Kantibhai Patell, the undercover bank clerk, who woke me, calling, "No!"

"You know who you're dealing with?" Bert snarled. "Do you know, you fuckin' wog terrorist?"

We did what we could. We had done it seventeen years before, when her parents had surprised us by waking to call her name from their bedroom. We kissed a dry-lipped panicky good-by. We gave each other addresses. I ran with her from the flat to the front courtyard to the corner at the bottom of the road—looking, always, for Barney and a machine-gun squad—where she would find a cab, with luck, and go to Brown's to tell lies. Or maybe she would tell the truth, I speculated: maybe the truths were what ignited Barney Korn. The last kiss was moister, her lips were warm, her tongue was cool, and I didn't want to let her go any more than I wanted her to stay.

I ran back up the hill to the apartment block, thinking of her voice, her tongue, the sounds we'd made, how far I'd come from my boyhood to my early middle-age—three and a half hours, I calculated—and then I was around the back as dusk poured in, to find Mister Halabi, Kantibhai Patell, dutiful *sub rosa* agent, behind the enemy's lines, stretched on his back and bleeding. I was panting too hard, and my legs felt too weak to hold me, so I didn't move toward Bert once I'd stopped, and I didn't speak. Halabi-Kantibhai Patell's blue-tinted glasses were unbroken on the flagstones beside him. They caught the bright last orange of the sun and darkened it. His right knee trembled, and his fingers opened and closed. The blood on the bridge of his nose and on his forehead was dark and bright, and what looked like a string of curdled milk was at the corner of his mouth. His breath sounded as though it bubbled up through water.

"Yes!" Bert called. In his dark blue shirt that was buttoned to the neck, probably his dusk-patrol uniform, he looked like a cop. The stubby silver wrench he thumped against his left hand threw reflections. "Yes, my friend," he said. "I told you I had my suspicions, didn't I? I'm not dead yet, and there's no fuckin' Arab killers coming into my flats in the dark of night to blow up the Jews in *my* parish. I decided to do a little early patrol is all it was, Jeremy. Toni thought she saw someone around the back. Oh, she's a ferret, she is."

Kantibhai Patell moved his head. I expected him to ask if a ferret was like a badger, and I bent, then, to put my hand beneath his sweaty hair.

"But I knew they'd come *some* night," Bert said. "I came around back here from the garage, and there he was. Crouching at your window, he was. He was just waiting. I didn't know for sure you were a Jew, Jeremy, until just now."

"Bert, this man—"

"I've sent for a panda car, Jeremy. They'll come in a minute and take him off for a little conversation."

"Bert, you could have *killed* him. And he's an Indian."

"Oh, this is no Indian, old son. You see that headgear I knocked off of him? What they call it in his country—"

His country, Bert's country, my country, Elaine's, and the country of the woman with whom I had lived. But the police car's siren sighed at the road in front of the building and, ever the man of profoundest research, the man of diligence, I sat on the flagstones next to Kantibhai Patell and looked, my eyes closed hard, at Bert, who was poised on the edge of his death, chiseled by light, protecting us all. I worked at how I would answer the authorities. It was because of professional labors, I would say. It was my business, I would have to say. It was because I was, like Kantibhai Patell, a trader. "Your word of honor," Bert reminded me, as Toni came running, and then the police.

THE SURGICAL WARD

ALLEN GROSSMAN

volo ut sis

I

"Go back along the track to the garden that surprised us
Turning us by an odor like a tone. I said, 'Look at the garden.'
And you said, 'I have never seen it before.'

                    Go back, and see
What is growing there now; how is the corn coming on?
Have the rumpled petunias survived the rain? Did they harvest
The snap beans on the fence?

               Go, look in the eyes of the garden.
With your brown eyes, look in the brown eyes of the garden.

II

If things have gone well, the garden will be almost harvested;
There will be some disarray. You said, 'It's nice how the flowers
And vegetables grow close together.'

               And I saw it was
A well-ordered garden, with plants of use and plants of beauty;

With low basil, and young fruit trees; and parsley and phlox,

poppies,

Strong vines and maize.

Leave your brown hair unknotted, as a favor.

The gardener was absent; but the mark of his strong hands was

III
In the brown hair of the garden. See how the garden has gone
Through its growth;

and whether the fragrance still prolongs its tone.

Go back, Patricia; and see the things there now I can imagine:
How the light falls from the lower sun; how the earth, where it
Was searched, is turned and moved; what flowers late, and what

will flower

Latest; and how the gourds lie close to the hand that will take

them. . . .

—The things I can imagine;

and the things, also, I cannot

IV
Imagine at all,

known but to you, of which I have no memory,
Only impotent guesses.

—The tone falters, and is dispersed in
The winter garden of what you see beyond our moment there,
Whither, as a last favor, I request you go,

by these

Long lines the tone prolonging some way into the silence
In which the gardener sleeps on the breast of the garden,
Strong hands at rest, refreshed of your brown hair and of your eyes,

V
Measuring and counting out, in his dream, another garden
With odor that will startle, and draw. . . ."

                            —"Dear Allen, what memory
Of those nights! Pain, fear, and the sense of death are heightened
In the dark.

              Walking the rounds by flashlight, between distress
Calls, and treatments—bottles of fluid draining into bodies,
Regulated the drop per minute, like water clocks;

                            and the quick needles;
Where once my hand hesitated, now a pattern of unbroken rhythm—

VI
I felt the strongest repulsion of death,

                            as the fetid smell
Of rotten flesh was labored out in the breathing of a man
Wasted by cancer,

                  who could communicate only pain. Then,
This last six A. M. all hell broke loose. He screamed, and in panic
Attempted to take off from his bed, pulled out his central I.V.,
And was covered with blood.

                        I learned, this morning, he had been
Taken to surgery. And now he is in the 'unit,'

VII
His bowel gone gangrenous. I do not think he shall get out.—

Perhaps it was 'the night effect'; I have never felt the repulsion
Of death so strongly physical.

                        —And later thoughts: *knowing* how
Little choice, still—*Let me die quickly!*

Well, I guess wishes
Are the place for creature privilege. There is not a jot of
Reason why I should escape the extremity that seems too much
The common lot; and yet. . . . Certain cries—are—of themselves."

VIII

"My dear, go back. Go back—there must be more. We were
astonished,
Patricia. It was a new thing. . . . But now in memory decays,
Confusing death's terror

with the favoring that brought to light the
Garden fragrant with a thunderous tone.

Go back. Abundance of low
Autumn light is on the vines; unknot your hair, and favor
With your brown eyes the eyes, and with your breasts

the small breasts
Of the garden. And say what is growing there now you see."

IX

"Allen, the morning air is crisp and clear. The leaves are brown.
I awakened feeling light. It is a day for the lady's pleasure.
The garden is unchanged,

silent and empty behind the hedge.
The autumn has not taken hold.

And I am mindful of the sun.
I like to think of you as when you are caught up in seeing.
Then perhaps you do not even know if you are

happy or sad;
But, then, you are very alive, and beautiful."

ELEVEN POEMS

GUNNAR EKELÖF

*Translated from the Swedish by Kenneth Rexroth
and Marcella Matthaei*

1 APOTHEOSIS

Give me either poison or dreams
either to live or to die
soon the ascent will arrive at the portals of the moon
already blessed by the sun
although the real has not yet married the dreams of death
they no longer have to weep for themselves

father I give to your heaven like a blue drop of the sea
the black world no longer inclines toward palms or psalms
but the winds of thousands of years comb the hair of the trees
the springs quench the thirst of the invisible traveler
vainly the four cardinal points turn around the bier
and by enchantment the angels' muslins
     turn into
     nothing

2

Night falls softly without wings
extinguishing the birds of the air
all the wings fall across the sun
silence opens the wind and the wings, the silence,
the rocks close up again
and gently extinguish the flowers
silencing the wind in the night and finishing the stones

> (when the transparent dream opens your eyes
> you live like flowers
> bending over stones)

3 TWILIGHT

The mother-of-pearl evening is lost in the ocean
all the countries of the world stretch far off under the surf
and the golden clouds beyond the horizon before me
behind me the tree frogs sing, little bells in the olive trees
the birds sleep in the white velvet sky
from which the wind pours over the sleeping waters
asleep before dreaming
the flowers asleep in the calm breeze of evening
in the gentle lullaby of the surf
together with the prophecies of the crickets
in the long twilight of half-closed eyelids
and the black eyelashes of the calm grasses
reflected in a pool of water

4 CHORUS

It was always the same
it will always be the same

just as the last man dreams fire
                it will all be over
just as our ultimate revolt to destroy ourselves
to break the circle and flee reality
to breathe deeply till we lose consciousness
                so deeply
that all the stars shine in our lungs
                to vanish northeast
                the calm face

5

I confess my belief
in the impossible,
its art is all the faith I have,
it is a false faith I confess.

I well know that here
it is the possible that matters.
Let me remain indifferent
to possible, to impossible, permit me.

Just as in the icons,
John the Baptist carries his head
intact on his shoulders at the same time
on a platter before him:
the sacrifice is no other than the sacrificer.
Me, I confess I believe
in the impossible
the art of experiencing
life and not being at the same time.

6 NIGHT

An eye rolls on the earth,
I twist myself so it can enter me.
The door is closed like lips,
the petal is heavy to carry.
The hair and the fingernails
quietly sprout in the silence.
The lips of the door are shut
on the disorder of riches.
There are no lights
under the eyelids of dream.
But toward the stolen
Comes the night and its thunder.

7

Like a spider web in the evening
soaked with dew
Like the road and the place it leads to
Like the disordered thicket which stops the wind
and the train roars and goes far away—
Oh nerves, why do you tremble
Memories, why do you swarm
Clouds, why do you soar
Loads, why are you so heavy

8

Five times I have seen that star
but the sixth time the moon comes out of the clouds
I do not try to escape
It hits me like the blow of an axe

so that I seem to twist my body
That you may read this

9

Who are you following me in the night?
What is your name?
Terror, deadly kiss,
miracle—
the flames of the sun burn me
and I am given to the vultures.
All night long
all the time my members
are scattered alongside the road

10

Paralyzed by the night—
the criminal—
having crawled a long time in the bowels of the Unconscious
as in this spherical room with its humid and slippery
walls covered with a net of red veins.
I have a confused sensation
of having found myself inside my own eyeball—
my eye which is opened for the first time

11 POETICS

You have to listen to the silence
to that silence we call formal perfection

that silence behind rhetoric
that silence behind allusions and elisions.
It is the quest of nonmeaning
in meaning itself
and reciprocally.
For all I have written with art
is properly without art
and all the full is empty.
And all that I have written
is found in the spaces between the lines.

SECOND SESSION ON THE COLOR OF THE SNOW

Stereophonic radio play for one voice

RÜDIGER KREMER

Translated from the German by Breon Mitchell

At the beginning of the play the voices are positioned as far as possible from each other—completely to the left and right of the stereophonic space. In the course of the dialogue the positions approach one another until—at the end—they overlap. The "questioner" is situated at an audibly greater distance from the microphone than the "answerer." This distance too diminishes in the course of the play. The approach of the positions toward each other should be so gradual and unnoticeable that the listener does not perceive it as an "effect." The points at which the positions should be contracted toward each other should be determined in discussion between the author, the speaker, and the director.

Good morning.

—Good morning.

Yes, come right on in. Sit down please. I'll be through in a minute. I'm just taking a quick run through the notes from our last conversation. We made a good deal of progress I thought . . . go ahead and light up!

Did you sleep well last night?

—yes . . . a deep and dreamless sleep. The pills you gave me helped a lot.

A proven remedy. We've used it for years, no side effects and absolutely dependable.

—why did you take the chess set away from me?

Oh, well, we didn't exactly take it away . . . let it go awhile. It will do you good.

—it was my only diversion . . . other than looking out the window at the garden.

I know—but it's only a temporary measure. It wasn't good for you to spend half the night pouring over the chessboard. I wouldn't have anything against your playing two or three games a day— perhaps with one of the attendants . . . old Mr. Vogel plays pretty well I think . . .

—no, I prefer to play against myself.

But you get all upset.

—no, it calms me.

I can't play chess—that is, I know how the pieces move of course, the bishops diagonally, the rooks straight ahead, the knights one forward one diagonal . . . but . . . I don't know, it all happens too slowly, and I lose the overall pattern, it makes me nervous, and then too I'm always furious when I lose a piece out of carelessness . . . at the same time I can imagine that it could be quite interesting . . . boring into the head of your opponent move by move . . . but when I try to imagine what it would be like playing myself . . . it just doesn't work: one player always knows in advance what the other has in mind . . .

—it's not always possible to know, it's possible to learn to shield your thoughts. Even against yourself . . . or more accurately, a point is reached where you no longer take sides . . .

Oh, come now, you have to take sides! For instance: black moves his knight in order to threaten check on the next move. The king has to move out of check and the knight takes the rook . . . but since you're both black and white at the same time you spot the trap and can make a countermove with white. So you have to choose between black and white!

—that's too simple—the way you're describing it—those are premeditated moves. I wouldn't sacrifice a rook lightly. (*Laughs*) Another principle is involved. In a normal game of chess—when two people play against each other—there's a winner and a loser . . .

Or a draw—no decision.

—a draw's out—a draw's no solution—a draw is defeat for both sides. In the past, when I—as you say, played "correctly"—I preferred to lose . . . whenever I could see that the game was going to end in a draw you might say I commited suicide.

Go on.

—There's nothing more.

Keep on talking, you wanted to tell me why you prefer to play against yourself.

—I didn't want to tell you anything. You asked me and I answered.

Yes, but you're the one who started talking about chess.

—I want my chess set back.

I ordered your chess set taken out of your room because I want you to sleep at night. When you sit in front of the chessboard half the night you're nervous and tense the next morning and can't concentrate on our conversations. And after all, we're not here to play chess . . .

—I demand an immediate explanation as to why I am being held here against my will. I demand to be set free immediately . . .

Now don't start with that again! We've discussed that time and again, and I really have to ask you to trust me. No one here wants to do anything to you. You've got to understand that—or simply believe it. And if you'll just help us a little we'll get where we're going in no time. It's not a matter of . . . Would you like some tea?

—yes, thank you.

Sugar?

—yes, thank you.

Lemon?

—yes, thank you, a few drops.

I think a few drops bring out the flavor too. People should really drink more tea. Coffee is just something you drink down, but tea you can really enjoy. I had a secretary once who was a real tea specialist. She kept five or six kinds of tea in her desk, orange pekoe, Earl Grey, green tea . . . god knows what all. It was a real ritual.

—At home, when I was a child, we always had tea, but that was different. My grandmother collected lime blossoms, blackberry leaves, elderberries, apple peels, mint . . . mostly we had mint tea, but when we got sick, or had a cold—then we had blackberry tea—or was it lime blossom?—I don't know. The white linen sacks were always hanging in the attic, lettered with laundry ink. When we were children the attic was our favorite place to play. I still remember when the Americans came, our mother hid everything in the attic—the radio, the camera, the binoculars, and my soldiers . . . I had a tremendous number of soldiers. My favorite one was throwing a hand grenade, you could see how the hand grenade—a stick grenade—was about to fly through the air . . . where it would land—a tiny toy explosion—it was too boring for the others, they were always boxing around with Dad's boxing gloves . . . but I could lie stretched out for hours playing with the soldiers . . . the only thing was I didn't have enough Tommies and Frenchmen, but there were even black soldiers among them. I had tanks and trucks, too, and an open commander's Mercedes with Hitler inside, you could raise and lower his arm, and when you lowered the arm then he had both hands at his side and looked terribly stiff and comical. One day my mother traded all my soldiers for a huge bundle of earmuffs. She unraveled them and knitted us all trousers and sweaters. They scratched horribly . . . I still can't wear wool against my bare skin to this day, and the smell of damp wool—is—simply—nauseating. There's nothing worse than sweating in a turtleneck sweater . . . the damp heat that's retained, the constriction—1 would rather freeze, be cold in general . . . I can stand cold much better than too much heat. . . . . . .

Do you feel better in the winter than in summer?

—How do you mean?

Oh, it's nothing important—it just seemed to me a bit . . . well, let's say "unusual" that someone would apparently prefer a cold dead season to the warmth of summer . . . when everyone loves the summer . . .

—how can you say something like "everyone loves the summer"?

You're generalizing . . . I don't know . . . if I had to choose be-
tween a crackling cold winter day, the air clear, so clear it hurts
your lungs, and the sort of sticky sultry summer day that takes
your breath away—even at night there's no relief . . . on days like
those I often dream of going to Patagonia.

Patagonia—why Patagonia?

—Oh, the word itself is so beautiful—Patagonia—it sounds like a
land that doesn't exist, a no-man's land with no one living there, a
land without streets, tramcars, and houses—only an airplane flying
over now and then high up in the ice-blue sky—silent—in total si-
lence . . . only the wind, the sound of the wind on the bare cliffs
and across the broad pure fields of snow. No trees and no blossoms,
only the smell of snow from the Antarctic—a totally pure land.
That's how I imagine Patagonia—even as a child I was enchanted
by it . . . (*Laughing*) Patagonia was in the very first poem I ever
wrote.

Can you recite it?

—Of course, after all it was my very first poem. I was seventeen or
eighteen years old when I wrote it . . . eighteen . . . my god
yes, then . . . then I knew what my life would be like: I was
going to be an author . . . no, a great writer . . . I would write
two books, both of them long true books about life, and then I
would die, young and unknown . . . like Lautreamont . . . there
wouldn't be any photographs of me and no definite dates . . . my
date of birth, entry into school . . . something like that of course,
but nothing else, no manuscripts and literary remains, just these
two books and perhaps a few drawings . . .

I don't want to interrupt you, but I would very much like to hear
the poem about Patagonia.

—It's not a poem about Patagonia—Patagonia occurs in it . . .
(*Amused*) it's a poem—so to speak, from my storm and stress
period:
they taught me
Pythagoras
Protagoras
Christianfürchtegottgellert
Patagonia   (with emphasis)
h two s o four

they didn't tell me
the rest

That's a good poem.

—You think so? . . . I think it's pretty good too, perhaps a bit presumptuous . . . precocious for an eighteen-year-old.
How did we get to it?

You were saying that you often thought about, that you often wished, to go to Patagonia.

—I mean—how did we get to Patagonia?

We were discussing your preference for coolness, coldness . . . and the attic where you played as a child. About the coldness in the attic.

—Yes, no matter how nice it was in winter—on winter days in the attic, I couldn't stand it in the summer, the gluey heat, stuffy with swirling dust . . . in the winter I always wore Dad's leather jacket—too bad in the end he cut off the epaulettes.

Epaulettes?

—Yes, the epaulettes.

Was it the jacket of a uniform?

—It was a black leather jacket with epaulettes with three silver stars on them. Whoever wore the leather jacket was the warder, the others were prisoners and had to do what the warder said.

What did they have to do?

—Whatever the warder said!

Well, what?

—The warder could bawl them out, they had to kiss his feet, or show their peepee . . . or let a handful of snow melt in their mouths—that really hurt your teeth . . .

Their peepee?

—Just kids' games, there was really nothing to it, the girls had to lift their skirts and the boys had to unbutton their flys and show . . . but the others were soon tired of it—they always boxed around then.

And you, what did you do?

—I played on by myself.

But if the others wouldn't play with you—I mean, you couldn't be warder and prisoner at the same time.

—Oh, that's simple enough. When you were wearing the black jacket you were the warder, and when you took it off you were the prisoner . . .

I see, but how could the prisoner carry out orders then . . . I mean, if you were both warder and prisoner, then one or the other couldn't . . .

—What do you mean? I could kiss my own feet, show myself my dick, beg myself for mercy, kick myself . . .

Tell me about the snow . . . tell me about the snow.

—You had to put it in your mouth and let it melt . . . you had to put a packed snowball in your mouth, bite down on it, and wait until it had melted.

But didn't that just kill your teeth?

—Of course it did, but that was the test!

Test?—Test of what?

—Or punishment.

Punishment for what?

—For being the prisoner and having to do what the black man said —or get your ears boxed, or kicked in the shins, or have to repeat.

Repeat what?

—I'm a dirty pig and I wet my bed, or my peepee stinks like a fish . . . and things like that . . . but why do you want to know that?

It's not really important—they were just the normal games of playing doctor, all children do it . . . but the bit about the snow: did you play the game only in the winter? Where did you get the snow—up there in the attic?

—That's very simple—now you think you can catch me in a lie . . . the snow stayed longest on the roof, all you had to do was open the attic window and there was soft white snow.

Yes of course, the snow was there, I wasn't trying to—as you say "catch you in a lie," that's nonsense, I just couldn't quite think for a moment how the snow . . . so there was soft white snow on the roof . . .

—Of course the snow crusted over and didn't pack so well during a thaw—and further up, on the ridge of the roof behind the chimney the snow was dirty from the smoke . . . there were snowrails running around the roof so that the snow didn't slide off . . . and there were two attic windows, one on each side, and there was a roof ladder too for the chimney sweep . . . I can't remember the exact number of rungs on it, but that shouldn't be of any great importance in judging my case!

No, please, there's no reason to get angry . . .

—I am not angry!

Irritated . . .

—I am not irritated, you keep insinuating things about me . . . you're always making insinuations . . .

Please, I'm sorry, I'm . . .

—always making insinuations that I'm not insinuating anything.

—not telling you the truth.

Didn't mean to insinuate anything.

—I demand that you apologize to me!

I've already said I'm sorry.

—In passing—only in passing, a turn of phrase, but not an apology.

Please accept my apologies.

—I accept your apology and request in the strongest possible terms that you cease doubting my statements. I have an excellent memory —it never fails me. I notice the smallest details: in April 1962—on our honeymoon trip—I played a game of chess with my wife on the train between Verona and Florence. She opened with the queen's gambit, and I took immediate advantage of her foolhardiness, placing her on the defensive from the first move, completely determined to take away every chance for development, forcing her into purely reacting. I could have checkmated her on various occasions. I let her feel that. But instead I forced her into a position where she couldn't move, I moved my bishop from D2 to G5. Instead of withdrawing her king to E4 she lost her head completely and moved her pawn to B4—one of my pawns was on B3. I moved my knight from A6 to C5—covering the squares E6 and E4 . . .

G4 was covered by my pawn on F3, G6 was covered by my rook on H6—that was it . . . Do you know what it means for a chess player to force his opponent into a position where he can't move? That is total victory, the total subjection of the opponent, a humiliation of his mind.

And?—how did your wife react?

—She tried to knock the pieces off the board—but it was a traveling set—the figures had small pegs on the bottom that you stuck in holes in the squares—they couldn't be knocked over. And I left the game set up—until Florence. We didn't say a word to each other— we simply stared at the board the whole time . . .
Is there any more tea?

Yes, help yourself.

—Would you like some more?

No . . . no, thank you.

—Now, are you convinced? Do I have a good memory?

Yes, you've convinced me, you have a very good memory.

—Well, thank you!

Tell me about the epaulettes.

—Dad came up to the attic one day and asked "What are you up to now?" and I said, we're playing Jews, and then he took his pocketknife and cut off the epaulettes and took them away . . . and without the epaulettes the game just didn't seem the same. He put them away in his nightstand then. I found them once when I was sick—when we were sick we were allowed to rest in our parents' bedroom. They lay there in a blue velvet case, behind the rosary and the aspirin—my father had headaches all the time . . .

You often complain of headaches yourself.

—If you mean by that—if you're trying to make some connection out of that, like I inherited that from Dad . . . I don't have any connection with my father, I take after my mother completely, around the eyes, and the mouth—even as a child everyone said I took after the Wessels—my mother's maiden name was Wessel—I am a true Wessel; my hair might be a little darker—but I'm taller than my brothers and sisters and have a straight nose—a narrow straight Wessel nose, that's obvious—I don't bear the slightest resemblance to my father. There are other reasons for my headaches. Bright light, oppressive weather, stuffy air, eye strain, insomnia—very concrete reasons.

What I'd like to know is why you came here . . . came back here to this city.

—My god, why'd I come back here?—I was a student here, I know the city—what do I mean "know"?—I've simply spent some time here, lived here, and wanted my wife to see it. After all those were important—decisive—years in my life.

Was your trip planned or spontaneous?

—What do you mean by planned—or spontaneous? I'd always wanted to show my wife the city sometime—but we never had—I never had the time— And suddenly I had a few days free—and so we took off—spontaneously, if you like.

How long did you live here?

—One year.

And when?

—Seven years ago—but you know all that, why do you ask?

Yes—I'd forgotten. —So you come here with your wife to show her the city. Was that your idea, or did your wife want to, I mean . . .

—It was probably more my wife's idea. I don't have very pleasant memories of my stay here; I'd told her a lot about it. You must know that I didn't—well let's say, feel quite right when I was here.

What happened?

—Pardon me?

Why didn't you feel quite right here—you stayed here a year after all.

—I had difficulties.

What sort of difficulties?

Personal difficulties.

Could you please explain them?

—I've already said they were personal difficulties. I don't want to talk about them—anyway they're not important.

I have before me a report from the central hospital. On March 12 you attempted suicide. You were admitted on the thirteenth. You remained under medical observation for four days . . . we can skip the medical details. You then spent four months under psychiatric care . . .

—Enforced.

What do you mean enforced?

—It's a very complicated story, I don't see why it still makes any difference after all these years. It's completely unimportant.

But there must have been a reason—a cause for it.

—There was no reason, and there was no cause.

What did you do on the twelfth of March?

—I got drunk and then by accident I took too many sleeping pills.

Just try to remember. What sort of a day was the twelfth . . . rainy? Sunny? Dull?

— . . . a thaw. Yes, there was a thaw. There were signs posted all over the city warning about roofslides. The sidewalks along the Burggasse were barricaded. A roofslide had killed an old lady . . .

So that morning you walked into town.

—Rode in—on the tram.

Go on!

That's all, I rode the tram into the city, walked around a little . . .

Were you at the university?

—I don't think so, by that time I had already stopped going there.

But . . .

—It bored me, it wearied me . . . literature of the Luther period and the history of the press since Bismarck . . . the exercises with selected examples.

We're getting sidetracked again. Let's start over at the beginning: you got up . . .

—Yes, of course . . .

You had breakfast . . .

—first I shaved and took a shower.

What did you have for breakfast?

—oatmeal with milk—as always.

What did you wear that day?

—I'm not sure anymore . . . yes, I do know exactly: I was wearing a blue-and-white-striped shirt, a gray pullover, jeans, and gray woolen socks . . . and a pair of undershorts. They were missing when they let me out of the hospital—and they had forgotten to bring along my shoes. I walked home through the city in my stocking feet . . .

All right, good . . . and then you rode into the city. Which line did you take?

—A 23 tram . . . listen, do you want me to tell you now whether the streetcar was crowded or empty, what color eyes the conductor had . . .

I want you to remember everything—try to remember every single detail.

—There's no such thing as total recall . . . haven't you ever lost a key you just opened the door with two minutes before, and then tried in vain to reconstruct those last two minutes?

Of course, but that's an entirely different matter . . .

—You're dusting your room and suddenly you don't know whether you've already dusted that chair or not . . . You either did something or you didn't, but you don't know which anymore . . . just a few minutes later!

That's why I'd like to try, with you, to discover what you did back then—as precisely as possible!

—I can only remember that day in general terms.

All right then, you were in the city, where?

—In the inner city. And then I had a cup of coffee in some coffee-house. And I watched the chess players . . . but I always did that.

Did you play too?

—No—but of course you play along when you're watching a game. I don't think it was a very good game, black gave up too quickly, tipped over his king and leaned back laughing in his chair—as if it didn't matter. But in fact his defeat could certainly have been avoided . . . I left then. But that could have happened on any day . . .

Go on.

—A bus for Schwarzenberg was standing at the bus stop, so I rode to Schwarzenberg.

. . . . . .

. . . . . .

. . . . . .

Was there any particular reason for that?

—No, the bus was standing there, I was bored—so I just took off for Schwarzenberg.

Had you been there before?

—No, that's why I went there, because the view of the city from the mountain was supposed to be so beautiful.

Tell me a bit about the trip and the visit . . .

—There's not much to tell. The bus was practically empty, a few tourists, two women sitting in front of me wrapped in black scarves. They seemed to be asleep. The road rises steadily in sharp curves. Two men were sitting behind me talking in whispers across the middle aisle. They spoke softly and quickly in a dialect so that I could only understand fragments of their conversation. However, it seemed—if I remember correctly—to have something to do with a case of murder. Then I fell asleep. The driver woke me. The bus was already completely empty. It had rained too. Then I went to the scenic point. But it was a very poor view. I stuck a coin in the automatic binoculars. But I couldn't see anything, not even the church spires of the city. I waited in a restaurant for the bus to leave and drank a few glasses of schnapps. I got sick on the way back—from the rocking of the bus and the bad air. And when we got back to the city it was already dark.

What did you do then?

—I went to a restaurant at the west end railway station and had something to eat.

Can you remember what you had to eat?

—Yes, of course, beef stew, that's what I always had there.

And then?

—Then I went to the movies . . . *Key Largo* with Humphrey Bogart and Edward G. Robinson.

You remember very precisely!

—You can't forget that film.

Why?

—Because it's one of the few films in which a story is really told to the end. It's going to end in death in any case, and you can bet on Humphrey Bogart or Edward G. Robinson.

Who did you bet on? Who did you put your money on?

—Oh, I don't mean really bet—it's actually clear from the beginning who's going to survive . . . all you can do is bet against yourself, because for yourself it's not at all clear . . . I mean if you are really involved in the film.

I don't understand.

—Whether you would shoot, whether you would have the nerve not to, for example.

Did you shoot?

—I don't know anymore—that changed from time to time. That's just the thing.

Oh yes—when you were in Kahlenberg . . .

—In Schwarzenberg!

In Schwarzenberg. When you were in Schwarzenberg, did anything happen?

—What would have happened? No, there was nothing—I already said, even the view . . .

Anything that might have shocked you?

—No! Nothing—I told you . . .

Frightened you? Confused you?

—I'm not saying anything more.

What was it about Schwarzenberg—that made you go back there this year?

—I haven't been there!

You were there!

—I'm not saying anything more!

I know that you were there. What happened in Schwarzenberg seven years ago . . . why did you go back there? Come on—tell the truth!

I want to hear the truth from you!

What happened?

All right. When you came out of the movies that evening you went home and got drunk . . . did that happen often?

Did you get drunk often?

And then you took sixty sleeping pills—just like that—no reason—by accident.

How did you manage that? You surely didn't just swallow sixty pills one after the other! You dissolved them in water—in tea? A big glass filled with milky fluid—it must have been a regular porridge . . . how did you picture yourself? As a hero? No, you hurt yourself. You hurt yourself badly—you wanted to strike out at the whole world . . . who did you want to punish? And when you had downed the stuff, how did you feel? Miserable, huh? Like a miserable dog . . .

—Stop it!

But you knew that your fellow lodgers would find you the next morning—set up a little drama—they would have knocked the next morning—to bring you the newspaper, to wake you up, or to bring the mail . . .

—Stop it!

All right what about it! The newspaper?

—We didn't get the newspaper.

The mail!

—I hadn't got any mail in a long time.

But you already knew your wife then, didn't you—didn't she write to you?

—No.

That seems very strange. You were living in different cities—far apart—and you didn't write to one another?

—Not back then.

Ah yes, not back then. And you gave up your studies—why?

—I've already told you, it bored me—I was fed up—I was fed up with it—I was fed up with everything—getting up in the morning, shaving—seeing myself in the mirror—my face—waiting for the mail that didn't come anyway, the cold room, the dark hall—the path,

always the same path from the room into the dark hall to the apart-
ment door and back—back and forth again and again in the sound-
lessness—the streets—you can't imagine how much I hate this city—
and the snow . . . you can't imagine how much I hate the snow—
the blinding white snow—the dirty black snow. Every morning
hoping it would finally thaw—but new snow had fallen overnight
. . . everything was blinding white. It hurt your eyes . . . my
eyes hurt terribly . . . and the east wind carried dust with it . . .
that coated the snow black, the snow looked marbled—looked
marbled—the horrible yellow piss-holes in the snow—and the blood.

Describe this photo to me!

Tell me what you see in this photo!

Tell me exactly what you see in this photo!

—A white VW. A white VW is standing in a field . . . in a snow-
covered field . . . The door on the driver's side is open . . . the
seat on the driver's side is tilted forward . . . a woman is sitting
in the back seat . . . her left leg is hanging out of the door . . .
her right leg is lying slightly bent on the driver's seat—on the tilted
back of the driver's seat. She's wearing boots that come up over
her calves . . . just short of the knees . . . her skirt is raised high
above her waist . . . she's wearing dark stockings with a black
border . . . and garters . . . you can't see the upper part of her
body and her head . . . she's probably asleep . . .

No, she's not asleep, she's dead—and now the other photo!

—My god!

Come on now—describe this other photo! . . . No, no, don't look
away, describe it—describe it just like you did the first one.

Come on now, it's a simple matter . . .
. . . you can see right away that she's dead . . .
. . . the way she's lying there . . .
. . . describe her face . . . !

—I can't describe her face . . .

Clever—there isn't much left of her face all right.
But the rest . . . Come on now!

—Her jacked is unbuttoned.

And her blouse?

—Her blouse is—unbuttoned too.

Unbuttoned? Look carefully!

—It's ripped open.

All right then. Unfortunately these are only black-and-white photographs. The boots are black, so are the stockings, the skirt and jacket are red, the blouse is again black . . . the VW is white . . . the snow-covered field is just above Schwarzenberg. The photos were taken on—just a moment—March 13th of this year . . . and now, let's have the whole story please!

—I could tell you practically any story you'd like to hear. I know a lot of stories, and often enough I don't know whether they're my own stories or stories from books, or stories from movies, or TV stories. It doesn't really matter anyway, all stories fit and they're all interchangeable, sometimes the index finger of my right hand actually crooks as if to fire a revolver, and I feel the point of contact, and my eyes are staring into the barrel of a revolver, and I see the scene in my mind in the movie where Humphrey Bogart is looking into the barrel of a revolver, and I have the same slight smile on my face. . . . . . I'll tell you what fascinates me about playing chess against myself: the inevitable chance to be the winner and the loser at the same time. And the snow—the snow isn't white like snow, the snow, the snow . . . sometimes you want to say a sentence that will change everything. And while you're thinking the words over, suddenly everything changes, and you have the feeling that you've been caught by surprise, you think now that you can say all the sentences you ever wanted to without feeling that these sentences have to change something. But the words don't come. You can't say the sentence. It's very sad, because suddenly the moment is past, all at once it's too late . . . but it's not really a matter of a sentence that will change everything. It's only a matter of the feeling that there might be a sentence . . . a sentence like that, that will change everything.

INSIDE OUT

JOHN TAGGART

To the reader: please read "Inside Out" out loud. Left to itself, the silent eye is confused and irritated by the poem. Its recurrences and substitutions are deliberately composed for the voice. In eye terms, the intent is a quality of light, of light that hovers, intense and complex, reaching out, taking in. In other terms, the intent is presence, the presence of these particular words, as the voice searches their interiors (but without violating them), turning them inside out that there may be community (exchange, embrace of interiors), singing, and dancing.—J.T.

1

You have to hear the sound before you play the sound.
You have to hear you have to you have to hear to
hear you have to give you have to give ear you
who have you who have ears you who have ears to
hear you have to give ear to hear the traveler you
have to you have to you have to give ear you who have
ears to hear the traveler who is a bird to
hear the traveler who is a bird who so sings.

If you call out to the bird and if you call out
to the bird and wait on the bird: the sound is there.

You have to hear the sound before you play before
you move before you move the hands before you move
with the hands you have to hear the sound before you
move before you clap before you clap with the hands.

If you call out to the bird and if you call out
to the bird and wait on the bird: the sound is there.

You have to hear you have to you have to hear to
hear you have to give you have to give ear you
who have ears you who have ears to hear
you have to give ear to hear the traveler to
hear the traveler who is a bird who is a bird who
so sings who is not visible who cannot be
handed about who is a bird who sings who is
a bird who is invisible who cannot be handed about.

If you call out to the bird and if you call out
to the bird and wait on the bird: the sound is there.

Before you move before you move the hands before
you move with the hands you have to hear the sound before
you move before you move with before you clap with the
hands before you clap with the hands for joy.

If you call out to the bird and if you call out
to the bird and wait on the bird: the sound is there.

You have to hear you have to you have to hear to
hear you have to give ear you who have
ears to hear you have to give ear to hear
the traveler to hear the traveler who
is a bird who is a bird who so sings who is
not visible who cannot be handed about who cannot

be broken who is a bird who is invisible
who cannot be handed about who cannot be broken.

If you call out to the bird and if you call out
to the bird and wait on the bird: the sound is there.

Before you move before you move the hands before
you move with the hands you have to hear the sound before
you clap before you clap with the hands for joy
before you move with the vibration in the air.

If you call out to the bird and if you call out
to the bird and wait on the bird: the sound is there.

You have to hear you have to you have to hear to
hear you have to give you who have
ears to hear you have to give ear to hear
the traveler who is a bird who is a bird who
sings who is not visible who cannot be handed
about who cannot be broken who is a bird who
is invisible who cannot be handed about
who cannot be broken who cannot be reassembled.

If you call out to the bird and if you call out
to the bird and wait on the bird: the sound is there.

Before you move before you move the hands before
you move with the hands you have to hear the sound before
you clap before you clap the hands for joy
before you move within the vibration in the air.

If you call out to the bird and if you call out
to the bird and wait on the bird: the sound is there.

2

You have to hear the sound before you play the sound.
You have to you have to you have to you

have to hear the bird who sings you have to hear the
bird out you have to listen to hear to
listen to the end to hear to the end to hear
the lesson to listen to the lesson to hear the
lesson to the end to listen to the lesson to
the end to hear out to attend and listen to the end.

The sound is there the sound is not there the sound
is there the sound is not: you will plead and sigh for it.

You have to hear the sound before you play before
there is room before there is room to clap
before there is room to clap and to pass around to
clap and to pass around and around to a great drum.

The sound is there the sound is not there the sound
is there the sound is not: you will plead and sigh for it.

You have to you have to you have to you
have to hear the bird who sings you have to hear the
bird out you have to listen to hear to
listen to the end to hear to listen to hear
to the end to hear the lesson to listen to the
lesson to hear the lesson to the end to listen to
the lesson to the end to attend and listen to the
end you have to depart to depart from all crowds.

The sound is there the sound is not there the sound
is there the sound is not: you will plead and sigh for it.

Before there is room before there is room to clap
to clap for joy you have to hear the sound
before there is room to clap and to pass around to
clap and to sway around and around to a great drum.

The sound is there the sound is not there the sound
is there the sound is not: you will plead and sigh for it.

You have to you have to you have to you
have to hear the bird sing you have to hear the
bird sing out you have to listen to the bird sing
out to listen to the end to hear the lesson to
listen to the lesson to hear the lesson to the
end to listen to the lesson to the end to attend
and listen to the end you have to depart from
all crowds to depart to depart from all friends.

The sound is there the sound is not there the sound
is there the sound is not: you will plead and sigh for it.

Before there is room before there is room to clap
to clap for joy you have to hear the sound before
there is room to clap and to pass and sway to
sway around and around with candles to a great drum.

The sound is there the sound is not there the sound
is there the sound is not: you will plead and sigh for it.

You have to you have to you have to you
have to hear the bird sing out you have to listen
to the bird sing out to listen to the end to
hear the lesson to listen to the lesson to hear the
lesson to the end to listen to the lesson to
the end to attend and listen to the end you have
to depart from all crowds you have to depart
from all friends to depart from all relatives.

The sound is there the sound is not there the sound
is there the sound is not: you will plead and sigh for it.

Before there is room before there is room to clap
clap for joy you have to hear the sound before there
is room to pass and to sway to sway around and
around as a candle dancer to a great drum.

The sound is there the sound is not there the sound
is there the sound is not: you will plead and sigh for it.

3

You have to hear the sound before you play the sound.
You have you have you have you have you
have to you have you have to you have to hear it
is you who have to hear the bird to hear the
bird you have to hear the bird sing you have to sit to
hear to sit under the singing to sit under the
singing of the bird to sit under the singing of
the bird in the court to sit in the court of the bird.

Allure the bird into the wilderness into the wilderness
that is yourself that the sound is there.

You have to hear the sound before you play before
there is room to clap you have to
hear the sound before you pass around sway around
as a candle dancer to a great drum as a source of delight.

Allure the bird into the wilderness into the wilderness
that is yourself that the sound is there.

You have you have you have you have you
have to you have to you have to hear it is you
who have to hear the bird to hear the bird you
have to hear the bird sing you have to sit to
hear to sit to hear to sit under to sit under the
singing sit under the singing of the bird to
sit under the singing of the bird in the court to
sit in the court of the bird to sit to hear to assent.

Allure the bird into the wilderness into the wilderness
that is yourself that the sound is there.

Before there is room to clap you have to
hear the sound before you pass around before you
sway around as a candle dancer to a great drum as
a source of delight as waves striking in the night.

Allure the bird into the wilderness into the wilderness
that is yourself that the sound is there.

You have you have you have you have you
have to you have to you have to hear it is you who
have to hear the bird to hear the bird you
have to hear the bird sing you have to sit to
hear to sit under to sit under the singing
sit under the singing of the bird to sit under
the singing of the bird in the court to sit in the
court of the bird to sit to hear to assent as in prayer.

Allure the bird into the wilderness into the wilderness
that is yourself that the sound is there.

Before there is room to clap you have to
hear the sound before you sway around as a candle
dancer to a great drum as a source of delight
as waves striking in the night as wind striking the waves.

Allure the bird into the wilderness into the wilderness
that is yourself that the sound is there.

You have you have you have you have you
have to you have to you have to hear it is you who
have to hear the bird to hear the bird you
have to hear the bird sing you have to sit to
hear to sit under to sit under to sit under the singing
of the bird to sit under the singing of the bird in
the court to sit in the court of the bird to
sit to hear to assent as in prayer being heard.

Allure the bird into the wilderness into the wilderness
that is yourself that the sound is there.

Before there is room to clap you have to
hear the sound before you sway as a candle dancer to

a great drum as a source of delight as waves
striking in the night as wind striking waves as cymbals.

Allure the bird into the wilderness into the wilderness
that is yourself that the sound is there.

4

You have to hear the sound before you play the sound.
It is you who have to hear it is you who have to hear it
is you who have to sit under the singing
of the bird it is you who have to sit in the
court of the bird to hear to assent to the
singing as in prayer being heard it is you who
have to sit in the court to assent
it is you who have to sit in a kind of silence.

The sound is there to turn inside out: what is
inside is not the bird not the bird but his presence.

You have to hear the sound before you play before
there is room to clap you have to hear the sound before
you dance as a candle as a candleflame as
a flame on the waves with your hair flowed back.

The sound is there to turn inside out: what is
inside is not the bird not the bird but his presence.

It is you who have to hear it is you who have to hear it
is you who have to sit under the singing of
the bird it is you who have to sit in
the court of the bird to hear to assent to the singing
to assent as in prayer being heard it is you
who have to sit in the court it
is you who have to sit in a kind of silence in
a silence in which the singing may endure.

The sound is there to turn inside out: what is
inside is not the bird not the bird but his presence.

Before there is room to clap you have to hear the sound before
you dance as a candle as a flame as
a flame on the waves with your hair flowed
back as a flame on the waves with your throat upturned.

The sound is there to turn inside out: what is
inside is not the bird not the bird but his presence.

It is you who have to hear it is you who have to hear it
is you who have to sit under the singing of the
bird it is you who have to sit in
the court of the bird to assent to the singing
as in prayer being heard it is you
who have to sit in a kind of silence in a
kind of silence in which the singing may endure in
which the singing only the singing may endure.

The sound is there to turn inside out: what is
inside is not the bird not the bird but his presence.

Before there is room to clap you have to hear the sound before
you dance as a candleflame as a
flame on the waves with your hair flowed back as
a flame on waves with your throat upturned in the night.

The sound is there to turn inside out: what is
inside is not the bird not the bird but his presence.

It is you who have to hear it is you who have to hear it
is you who have to sit under the singing of the bird it is
you who have to sit in the court of
the bird to assent to the singing as prayer
being heard it is you who have to
sit in a kind of silence in a kind of

silence in which the singing may endure in
which the singing only singing may endure in you.

The sound is there to turn inside out: what is
inside is not the bird not the bird but his presence.

Before there is room to clap you have to hear the sound before
you dance as a candleflame as a flame on
the waves with your hair flowed back as a flame with
your throat upturned burning in the night.

The sound is there to turn inside out: what is
inside is not the bird not the bird but his presence.

EIGHT POEMS

GABRIEL ZAID

Translated from the Spanish by Eliot Weinberger, Margaret Randall, and Carlos Altschul

THE MURMUR OF WATER IN THE FOREST

We made
ephemeral
poems

with laughter   with a glance

drunk
like Li Po

releasing eternity

There they go

leaves   rhymes
of eyes   of laughter

The freedom   The Joy
of the eternal   of never
without return   recuperating

[EW]

SONG FOR THE SAME

The same is so satisfying!
To discover the same.
To relive the same.

The same is so tasty!
To lose yourself in the same.
To find yourself in the same.

Oh ineffable same!
Give us always the same.

[EW]

SUN ON THE TABLE

God is here.
Lost in the depths
of an obvious
glass of water.

God is here.
The breeze, the sun, the table,
are not God. My eyes
are not God.

God is here.
The window shook
and the Holy Spirit
danced in a glass of water.

[EW]

DEADLY EXERCISE

Pull in the oars and drift afloat
with your eyes closed.

Open your eyes and know again
your life: the miracle repeats.

Go on, get up and forget
this hidden shore
you've landed on.

[MR]

SURF

The sun bursts
         and crumbles
to renew itself in your abandon.
Waves burst from your breast.
I bathe in your laughter.

Waves, clouds and suns
and beaches overflowing.
Your laughter is Creation
happy to be loved.

[MR]

EVOLUTION

Grace went searching for the first couple
who dared to open their eyes
in the eden of being alive.

[MR]

MOONLIGHT

Naked beasts that night nurses.
Zebras closing the blinds.

Sad panthers in their cages.
Twins in the kangaroo of bed.
Owls: each one its lamp.

[CA]

GUSTS OF WIND

Death takes the world to its windmill.

Sunsails in the thunderclouds
brought in unreality,
presaged the end of the world.

Your laughter
spun daisies
in the darkness of your throat.

Your imperfect teeth
shed its petals
as you offered your breasts to the rain.

Your heavy skirt spun
like foliage you pressed,
tree heavy with memory
after the rain.

You were drenched. You laughed,
while I longed for your white
bones like laughter
on the troubled end of the world.

[CA]

ALPHABET OF REVELATIONS

WALTER ABISH

1

The new occupant of 26 Sustain Drive unloaded the battered blue
Ford panel truck with the Arizona plates, and then, without seek-
ing anyone else's assistance, she awkwardly (how else) lifted and
carried the half-dozen cardboard boxes, one by one, into the house.
Although Brooks must have known that she was being observed
from across the street, she did not once look up, since to do so in
all likelihood would have involved her in a possible exchange with
whomever had been patiently following her activity from the mo-
ment she first got out of the car.

A few days after her arrival Bud and Arlo observed her at work
in the small garden. Arlo had spotted her first and abruptly stopped
the car in the middle of the road just where it began to slope
downhill. She's got a determined sort of look, wouldn't you say,
Bud asked, but Arlo did not comment. Remaining indifferent, it
seemed, to their presence, she continued watering the lawn,
patches of which had turned a faded yellow. Afterward she picked
up a pair of clippers, and with her back to them, inexpertly, at least
to their eyes, trimmed the hedge at the back. Arlo kept drumming
his fingers on the steering wheel until Bud wanted to tell him to
stop, because the sound was affecting his concentration.

All in all, the people who now and then pulled up in their cars
to observe, furtively or not, the somewhat stocky young woman

with the shoulder-length blonde hair, did so, or so it would appear, in order to ascertain to what extent she differed from them, or the people they knew, for a difference was clearly indicated. It was, however, impossible to determine the precise nature of that difference. It was impossible to tell without a closer examination, for instance, of the interior of the house, without a look into one of those heavy sealed cartons stacked neatly in the small room next to the kitchen, or a glimpse of the framed reproduction by the Belgian painter Magritte (1898–1967), entitled *Alphabet of Revelations*, now hanging in what was the Reverend Gleiss Pod's former living room.

Did Arlo really tell Clem, in confidence, that he intended to obtain a better and clearer picture of Brooks's expectations and needs.

Seventeen years ago when the Secaucus River overflowed, three people were drowned, the Kienhover Bridge, named after a German musicologist (1885–1957), collapsed, four thousand tons of cement stored at the Bugano and Lead warehouse were transformed into one massive immovable rock, and the entire row of thirty-two houses on Sustain Drive, eighteen of which overlooked the river, stood—depending on whether they were on the south or north end of the drive—under two to six feet of muddy water for seven days. Having lost his parents and his baby sister, Fabric, to the Secaucus River, Arlo, now an orphan, moved out of 26 Sustain Drive to live with his aunt and uncle seven blocks away at 84 Dolchinger Lane. Each day on his way to school Arlo would make a slight detour to pass his former home and see how the new occupants, a Reverend Pod, who had been a missionary in China, and his daughter, Klairdine, were coming along. Eight years later the two magnificent elm trees in front of 26 Sustain Drive had to be cut down, and the true state of neglect of the house could no longer be hidden from view. In 1975 the Reverend Pod and his thirty-one-year-old pregnant daughter slipped away late one night without so much as a word to any of their neighbors. Arlo confided to Bud that he was the father of Klairdine's baby. Bud told Clem, who in turn mentioned it to his wife, Donna, who said that she wasn't in the least bit surprised.

2

Now number 26 was the only building without an air conditioner in any of the windows, or a TV antenna on the roof. It was, furthermore, the only house with a mailbox that did not bear the name of the present occupant. Why? The Kufflers in 24, the Altmeers in 28, the Mungalls across the street in 25 had no such compunctions. What was Brooks trying to conceal? Was she not the sole occupant, or didn't she expect any mail?

It sure needs a coat of paint, Bud whispered to Arlo as they crouched behind the mangled hedge at the rear of 26, hoping to catch a glimpse of Brooks.

It also needs complete rewiring, said Arlo, settling himself comfortably on the grass. And what's more, the balcony isn't safe. I remember being at a party over here late one night five or six years ago, and finding myself on the balcony with a certain young lady, a close friend of Klairdine.

Do I know her? Bud inquired.

You bet. You married her.

I'll be damned, said Bud softly.

But why has Brooks moved here? Here, meaning to New Jersey, to number 26, a two-story frame building that might any day now decide to slide into the Secaucus River.

To their chagrin Arlo and Bud did not catch a glimpse of the occupant of 26 Sustain Drive that evening. We'll catch her on our way to work tomorrow, Bud promised. Arlo nodded, trying to conceal the extent of his disappointment.

By and large Arlo and Bud were convinced that they more or less knew what a woman could and couldn't do. Still, something about Brooks filled them with an uncertainty. Why the Arizona plates on her car? Was she expecting someone to join her? Could she be hiding someone in the house? Why didn't she smile like everyone else and wave her hand casually in response to a greeting?

Arlo and Bud were acutely aware of all the things a woman could do.

She can run up a flight of stairs
sew on a button
prepare a spinach pie for seven
toss a vase across the room
correctly set the dial on the old washing machine in the cellar
and determinedly search for a word in the dictionary, a word that
would spell a certain release, a word that would contribute to light-
ening the burden people feel suddenly, when they least expect it,
in their hearts, or roughly in the area where they suspect their
hearts to be, somewhere below the left shoulder, and a bit to the
right. She can also with a look of alarm sit up in bed and ask:
Where have you been? Where have you been?

On their return to 26 Sustain Drive, Arlo and Bud carelessly left
their footprints on the flower beds beneath the first-floor windows,
and then, equally careless, neglected to wipe their fingerprints off
the kitchen window ledge at the back, and off the doorknobs, the
table top, the banister, the pile of unopened boxes, the upstairs
closet, and the chest of drawers. They even examined the contents
of the medicine cabinet in the bathroom. No lipstick anywhere,
Bud pointed out matter-of-factly. Or any of the stuff Faye uses on
her face. I used to sleep in there as a child, Arlo said, pointing to
the small room, now completely vacant, to the left of the staircase,
the tears welling up in his eyes. Can you believe it? They haven't
even changed the green wallpaper. It's the same wallpaper.

3
But they are my buddies, Clem earnestly explained to Donna. We
spent a year in Vietnam. We stuck together in L.A. We were
busted in Las Vegas, and then the following year we drove to
Florida. I introduced Faye to Bud and Erna to Arlo. I won't have
you saying all those things about them. For one thing, you can't
prove it. For another, it's simply not true.

She watched him as he bent to pick up the pieces of the shat-
tered yellow glass pitcher she had thrown at the turquoise living
room wall.

I think I am going to watch the late late movie tonight, she
announced.

I wish you wouldn't let yourself get carried away by every little thing, he said, still bent over, peering at the floor, searching for tiny pieces of yellow glass he might have overlooked.

Did Brooks, the new occupant of 26 Sustain Drive, ever discover the footprints of Arlo and Bud in the flower beds beneath her first-floor windows?

4

Yesterday Donna smashed a yellow glass pitcher against our living room wall. I ducked just in time, said Clem. That pitcher cost fourteen ninety-five. But he neglected to tell Arlo and Bud the reason for her outburst, and they were too polite to ask. The waitress distributed clockwise the familiar stained menus in their plastic jackets. Bud noticed the slight tear in her white blouse, just beneath the left arm-pit. Stretching to take something down could have caused it. Clem ordered the fried shrimp and French dressing on his salad and a Budweiser. Bud ordered a veal cutlet, but not like the one he had last time with too much breading, mashed potatoes, no salad, and a Schlitz, and Arlo kept the waitress waiting because he could not make up his mind. He could not decide what he really wanted. How's the liver today? He looked at her expectantly.

Bud waited for her to leave and then said that in Clem's place he would be firm with Donna. Very firm, he stressed, one eyebrow raised and his forefinger planted on the Formica table top.

Clem laughed. She could have picked something less fragile to toss at me . . .

Arlo interrupted to say that he was planning their next trip upstate.

I'll join you guys, Clem said, but only if Bud promises not to bring any guests along.

Bud raised his hand as if taking an oath. I promise, I promise. I only asked Keller to join us because I heard a rumor that they were going to promote him to section chief.

I don't like Keller, said Clem.

He still lives with his mother, said Arlo, and then seeing the waitress asked her if it was too late to change his order of fried liver to the asparagus omelet.

While unpacking Brooks dropped a large white serving plate with a blue rim. The plate smashed on impact. The man who had come to install the telephones rang the front doorbell just as she was sweeping up the pieces.

She's the unfriendliest woman I've ever met, the telephone man later told Clem. She now has a Princess phone in the upstairs bedroom and two Touchtones downstairs, one in the living room, the other in the kitchen. At first she couldn't decide on the colors. She finally picked white for the Princess, blue for the living room, and black for the kitchen. Imagine, black for the kitchen.
Does she appear to be by herself? asked Clem.

5
The blue Ford panel truck in Brooks's driveway still had the Arizona plates. No one on Sustain Drive had ever been to Arizona. No one on Sustain Drive had the slightest inkling where Brooks worked or, indeed, if she worked at all. Mr. Mulhout, the owner of the hardware store on Bush Street, told Donna that Brooks had purchased a lawnmower the day before. She also bought four gallons of white latex, a fly swatter, a dozen storm windows, an aluminum stepladder, an electric drill and bits, fifty pounds of plaster, and a tube of epoxy.
Did she mention Arizona? Donna wanted to know.

Why don't we ask her over one night, Clem suggested.
I don't think she's very keen on people, Donna replied. When she first moved in I rang her bell and asked her if she needed anything. She said no. She didn't even smile. Now I no longer greet her.
Well, ask her over anyway.
We could also invite Arlo and Erna, and Bud and Faye.
Despite what you think of them?
Despite what I think of Arlo and Bud.
Damn it, there's another stain on my carpet, yelled Clem, absolutely livid with anger. Did you know that? You didn't tell me that you had spilled something on my carpet.
If it's so important to you, take it to the cleaners.
Do you have any idea how much that carpet cost?

Well, will you call Brooks, or shall I, asked Donna.
You call her, said Clem.

6

I still can't believe it, said Erna as she and Donna entered the new mall. Two months ago I had to drive twenty miles in order to get a decent pair of shoes. Do you know that Clem is absolutely lost without me, said Donna. He can't even pick out a shirt for himself. He needs my approval for everything he does. Arlo won't let me buy a thing for him. He always seems to know exactly what he wants.

Well, as long as he knows.

Don't make me laugh, said Erna.

I am not afraid of you, said Brooks, speaking slowly and evenly into the telephone. I'm not in the least bit afraid of either of you. But I am getting sick of hearing your heavy breathing, you degenerates.

She knows, Arlo said miserably. Damn it, she knows.

I am thinking of getting Clem some darts and a dartboard for his birthday, said Donna. He has his heart set on a pinball machine, but they're over three hundred. Did you know that Clem, Bud and Arlo are planning their next little trip to the woods?

They just got back.

Erna smiled grimly. Well, if that's what makes them happy.

I know what makes me happy, said Donna. She looked at Erna, who laughed.

Arlo and Bud were aware of all the things a woman could do.
She can run up a flight of stairs
mend a torn sleeve
plan next day's dinner
sit up in bed
with a startled look
and ask:
Where have you been?

Does one ever lose the need to be desired? Donna asked Erna. They had each just bought a pair of Swedish clogs and were headed for the Angkor What? Restaurant and Cocktail Lounge. I can't bear to be alone at night, Donna told Erna as they were wait- ing for their second Angel's Kiss. Each time Clem has the night shift, I stay up till three watching TV. From where they were seated they had an unimpeded view of the shoe store and the candy store next to it, and the Valley Savings & Loan Association and the health food store and a large fountain into which shoppers would occasionally throw pennies.

At a nearby table a woman their age said to her friend: I just don't understand it Everyone except me has been invited to the party. I don't understand it.

It's an oversight, said her friend, staring at Erna who was wear- ing her new pale-green backless dress. Erna told Donna that Bud was beating Faye. I promised Faye that I wouldn't tell anyone. Bud keeps complaining that she doesn't know how to run their house.

Well, he's right you know, said Donna.

Still, that's not reason enough to beat her.

Donna laughed. Clem would never hit me. He wouldn't dare.

As they left the restaurant, Erna spotted Arlo in a phone booth. I was just calling you, he said sheepishly when he came over.

But I told you that I was going shopping.

Didn't you say that you'd be back by three?

I didn't. But what are you doing in the mall?

I was just passing, and I thought I'd pick up a pair of stereo headphones.

Don't believe a word they say, said Erna gaily.

Why, there's Brooks. Does she always wear jeans?

What's for dinner, Arlo asked Erna, who was unpacking groceries in the kitchen.

Fried liver, she said, and then told him that his best friend Bud was beating Faye.

She's such a lousy homemaker, he explained. Their place is al- ways a mess.

I wish I really knew what you want, Erna said.

He looked at her in surprise. Why do you keep asking me? I think I want to be good at what I am doing. I'd like to be section supervisor in a year or two. I also would like to buy a larger house in a place like Dumont. And, I guess, I also want pleasure.

How do you mean, pleasure?

Well, you know—gratification. To excel.

Sex?

Yes. That also.

At night, as she undressed, she said: Don't you ever wish to share your thoughts with me?

7

I am still surprised that Brooks accepted our dinner invitation, said Clem. She really gets under my skin.

Why, asked Donna.

I don't know. I keep asking myself, but I don't know.

I know why, said Donna. It's because she fails to respond to your charm. Because she doesn't laugh when you describe your hunting accidents. Because she's not interested. Period.

Would you just tell me one single thing, said Clem. Why doesn't she invite anyone to her place.

Clem could not miss the triumphant look on her face when she said: She's invited me in to have a drink.

Well?

Well what?

Well, why doesn't she ask anyone else?

She's asked me.

She hasn't asked us, said Clem. She hasn't asked Arlo, or Bud, or me.

When Clem and Donna separated, she kept the Moroccan rug and the large oak bookcase with the built-in liquor cabinet, the new leather couch and the leather armchair and the marble-topped coffee table, the Panasonic stereo, but he took the Zenith color TV, the Remington electric typewriter, the station wagon, the garden tools, and the framed reproduction of Paul Delvaux's *Eloge de la Mélancholie*.

Donna also kept the movie projector and the Super-eight movie camera, the water bed and the garden hose, the linen and all the director chairs. He took the miniature lathe, the electric saw, and the ten-speed racer he had bought for her birthday. She let him have the terra-cotta figurine of Chalchiuhtlicue the river goddess she had picked up in Mexico, and he left her the massive Ronson table lighter, a gift from his favorite aunt, Mabeline, who lived in Paris, Iowa. He also left her the new dartboard. She came close to tears when he left.

When Arlo and Erna separated, Erna kept the seventeen-inch Sony color TV and the Toyota and the house and the two-year-old baby, but he took Class, the three-year-old bulldog he had given her on their first wedding anniversary in May 1975. He also took the stereo and the entire record collection except for an original movie soundtrack of *Plead for Love,* with Rick Jordan and Audrey Su. She helped him load the rented van. It was, as these things go, an amicable parting. They even asked Brooks to join them for a drink. Since he had packed all the booze, they drank tomato juice with a dash of bitters. Brooks mentioned that she intended to visit her uncle, who had a farm in upstate New York. Erna caught the instantaneous flicker of interest on Arlo's face. Upstate? I have a lot of friends upstate. That's where Bud, Clem, and I go hunting. Whereabouts upstate?

8

Each time Donna watered the snapdragons, the zinnias, the caladiums, the marigolds in her tiny garden with the green hose Clem had left behind, she was reminded of Clem who, barefoot and wearing his torn jeans, had always spent half an hour each day casually directing a stream of water at one, then another section of the garden while dreamily staring into space. Why did you have to break up with him, her mother kept asking her whenever she called.

When old Mr. Mulhout sold his hardware store on Bush Street, Donna bought a rake, a hammer, three pounds of two-inch nails, a pair of pliers, and a birdfeeder, all at a twenty-five percent discount. What are you going to do, now that you've retired, she asked

Mr. Mulhout. I'll move to Florida, he said. I've sold my house and all my furniture. I intend to sell my car. I'll move to St. Petersburg. I may marry again. Are you interested in buying a two-year-old air conditioner?

How many BTUs? she asked.

He looked terribly upset. I don't remember. I don't seem to remember anything any longer.

I know it's absolutely insane, but I loved that rug I picked up years ago in Morocco, Clem told Erna, when he ran into her on Palisade Avenue. I'd give anything to have it back.

I'll mention it to Donna, Erna promised. She might let you have it.

I really hate to be tied to possessions, he remarked. It's a weakness.

As long as you acknowledge it to be a weakness, it stops being one, she said.

When Bud, who also lived only a block away from the Secaucus River, left Faye, he broke all the front windows. He took her fur coat and the Tiffany lampshade. He also took the two air conditioners, the cameras, the movie projector, the freezer, the refrigerator, and the two-by-three-foot photograph of him and Faye, arm in arm on a beach in Mexico. He moved while she was at work in the beauty parlor. He moved everything but the wood shutters and the plants in the garden. When he left the house he felt sorry that there was not anything else that he felt tempted to take.

Can I stay in your place tonight? Faye asked Brooks when she returned to the empty house. She instinctively called Brooks, because Brooks seemed so terribly independent. Sure, said Brooks. Come on over. I am going to see my uncle in a few days, but you can stay here until I leave.

9

When Clem, on an impulse, called Donna to inquire if she would mind terribly if he would come by and pick up the water bed, which he had bought, she said sure, by all means. It took Clem only half an hour to empty the water from the water bed. The most expedient way of getting rid of the water was to stick the end of the hose, the familiar old green hose, out of the bedroom window. Brooks, who was passing their house, could not understand the reason for all that water gushing out of the bedroom. Hi there, Brooks, Clem called to her when he looked out of the window to see if the flow of water was being obstructed by anything. How are you Brooks? Is there anything else you would like to take, now that you are here? Donna asked Clem. He wanted to ask her about the Moroccan rug, but his courage failed him. Had she given it away? It was not in the living room or in the bedroom.

When Brooks passed the house later that afternoon she heard Donna moaning. It was summer and the windows of the bedroom were open. The sounds were quite loud and unmistakably sexual. Brooks, lost in thought, kept standing beneath one of the windows, as each moan mounted and subsided, forcing in her brain a curious standstill of all thought and recognizable emotion.

Whenever Erna and Donna met they did not discuss Arlo or Clem or Bud and his terrible treatment of Faye. Erna noticed that Donna had made a substantial number of changes in her house. There was a new teakwood china closet and a new green glass-topped coffee table near the velvet sofa. How's the baby doing, Donna asked. I'm so glad it's a girl, said Erna. I am looking forward to watching her grow up. Where is she? asked Donna. Oh, my mother in Freehold is taking care of her. Did you know that Brooks belongs to a gun club in New Jersey, and that I am thinking of joining? Whatever for, asked Donna. For self-protection. I don't want whatever happened to Faye to happen to me.

10

The four of them set off early Saturday morning in Donna's car. When they drove past the park where Donna had first met Clem, she said, I don't have the slightest idea where he is staying. I don't even care. I wonder if something is seriously the matter with me?

You'll like my uncle, said Brooks. He was the best shot in Carefree, Arizona. He taught me to shoot, and he'll teach you.

Near Albany they had a flat tire. Nothing to it, said Brooks. They stood watching her as she changed the tire, admiring her dexterity and her self-confidence. It took them less than forty minutes to get back on the road and another hour and a half to reach the farm. It's nice to have you visit, said Brooks's uncle when he met them at the gate. He was wearing an old tweed hat and a beat-up jacket.

Brooks introduced them: This is Erna, and this is Donna, and this is Faye. You remember my mentioning Faye to you?

After lunch, which they ate in the large kitchen, Brooks's uncle took them to the make-shift rifle range at the back of the barn. While her uncle looked on, Brooks showed them how to load, aim, and fire the rifle they had first seen on the wall above the fireplace in the living room. There's a little bit of a kick when you press the trigger, Brooks said, but you'll get used to it.

At night Erna, who was sharing a room with Donna, said to her friend: I'm not sure if you noticed, but I think Brooks's uncle is really a woman dressed up as a man.

Are you serious? asked Donna. Why should Brooks's uncle be a woman? It doesn't make any sense.

I know it doesn't make sense. But I'm pretty certain.

How do you know?

She's a woman. I just know.

Are you going to mention this to Brooks?

No, should I?

I guess if she doesn't, there's no reason to.

Well?

And Donna, from where she lay on the bed, hands folded behind her head, staring at the ceiling, complacently said: Well, you may be right. But did you see how well she can shoot. Each shot, a bull's eye.

THE SERMONS AND PREACHING
OF THE CHRIST OF ELQUI

NICANOR PARRA

Translated from the Spanish by Edith Grossman

—AND NOW JUST FOR YOU

Our Lord Jesus Christ in person
who after 1977 years of religious silence
has graciously agreed
to attend our gigantic Holy Week program
delighting both young and old
with his wise and timely ideas
O. L. J. C. needs no introduction
he is known throughout the world
just think of his glorious death on the cross
followed by a resurrection no less spectacular:
a round of applause for O. L. J. C.!

—Thank you for the applause
even though it's not for me
I'm an ignorant man but not an idiot
there are some speakers
who'll do anything
just to get cheap applause
but I forgive them

they're only innocent jokes
although that's not the way it should be
seriousness is better than kidding around
especially when you're dealing with the gospel
it's just fine if you laugh at me
it wouldn't be the first time
but not at O. L. J. C.
that's what decent people will say. (applause)

   I
Even though I come prepared
I really don't know where to begin
I will begin by taking off my glasses
don't think that this beard is recent
I haven't cut it for 22 years
and I haven't cut my fingernails either
in other words I have kept my vow
longer than I had to
the obligation was only for twenty
I haven't cut my beard or fingernails
only my toenails
in honor of my beloved mother
but for that I had to suffer
humiliation slander scorn
and the truth was I didn't bother anybody
I was only keeping the sacred promise
that I made when she died
not to cut my beard or nails
for a period of twenty years
in homage to her sacred memory
to renounce ordinary clothing
and wear humble sackcloth instead
now I will reveal my secret to you
the penitence is over
soon you will be able to see me
dressed as a civilian again.

II

The 5th of February 1927
I was working in the north
as a laborer for a master mason
contracted to an American company
anxious to earn a little money
to help out my folks
they were in terrible shape
she was confined to bed
and the old man was unemployed
when I heard my name
                    on the p.a.
I felt my blood
                    run cold in my veins
even though the heat was suffocating
naturally I suspected the worst
and sad to say I was right
I must have lost my mind
at first I laughed
I couldn't believe my eyes
my God it's impossible—it can't be true
I tore up the telegram in despair
and when I was myself again
I sat down on a rock to cry
                    like a baby
forgetting that now I was a man
                    a real man.

III

When they saw me dressed in this humble sackcloth
even the priests made fun of me
they who should have set an example
they're not God's representatives on earth
                    for nothing
I'm absolutely certain
that He would not have made fun of me
everything was in honor of a mother
how could I do anything else

while she was sleeping her eternal rest
imagine her son enjoying himself
with loose women
it would have been an unforgivable betrayal
considering that I was her only son
a man and not a god as some people believe.

IV
Let no one say that I'm a beggar
if he doesn't know how I've earned my own way
in the 20 years since I made my promise
traveling the length of the country
neighboring countries too
preaching sound doctrine
for the good of Mankind
although reasonable men called me crazy
hundreds of lectures in prisons and hospitals
in Old Age Homes
in Benevolent Societies
I was not born for self-glorification
I was born to help my brethren
especially souls in torment
without regard to social class
evicted invalids
or persons of scant means
never accepting charity
it has been the same old story
humiliations mockery laughter
when they saw me dressed in humble sackcloth
there were weeks months even years
when I couldn't find a place to sleep
no one wanted to give me lodging
I was earning enough money
with the sale of my modest little books
(to date I've published 18)
more than enough to pay for a hotel
and nevertheless they turned me away
with one excuse or another

although I would have paid twice the regular rate
if it hadn't been for the Chilean police
I don't know what would have happened to me.

V

A drunk once
dared to pull my beard
but my will power triumphed
and I remained absolutely still
not a muscle of my face moved
and the attacker had to withdraw
without enjoying the fruits of his insult
he was hoping that I would be insulted
and that he could have a good laugh
that's why I say in my lectures
that virtue must come before everything
so that no one will suffer unjustly
seriousness and patience come first.

VI

Some advice of a practical nature:
early to rise
eat a light breakfast
a cup of hot water is enough
don't wear tight shoes
avoid socks and hats like the plague
meat two or three times a week
I'm a vegetarian but not a fanatic
don't make the mistake of eating shellfish
everything from the sea is poison
don't kill birds except in the case of extreme necessity
avoid alcoholic beverages
one drink at lunch is sufficient
no more than 15 minutes siesta
just losing consciousness is enough
sleeping too much is harmful
don't retain wind in your stomach

you can burst an intestine that way
sexual abstinence during Holy Week
*zahumerio** every two weeks
completely white underwear
except when your mother dies
given the extreme gravity of the situation
you should wear strict mourning
when I had to go through that traumatic experience
(I wouldn't wish it on my worst enemy)
I decided to dress completely in black
from the inside out
and that's what I've been doing for 20 years
from that fateful day to this.

VII

Husbands should really take a correspondence course
if they don't have the courage to do it in person
on the female genital organs
there is too much ignorance in this matter
for example who among them could tell me
what the difference is between the vulva and the vagina
and yet they think they have the right to marry
as if they were experts in the field
and the result: marital problems
adultery slander separation
and what happens to the poor children?

VIII

I am more herbalist than magician
I don't solve problems that can't be solved
I cure I calm people's nerves
I make the devil leave their bodies
I really lay into it when I lay on hands
but I don't revive rotting corpses

* Less than exorcism, more than mere burning of incense, *zahumerio* (or *sahumerio*) is a semireligious, semisuperstitious burning of aromatic herbs for the purpose of physical and spiritual purification.—E. G.

the sublime art of resurrection
belongs exclusively to the divine master.

IX

Now that I have revealed my secret
I should like to say good-bye to all of you
at peace with myself
and with a warm embrace for you
because I have successfully completed
the mission that God entrusted to me
when he appeared to me in dreams
22 unhappy years ago
I swear I feel no rancor toward anyone
not even those who questioned my virility
let those honorable gentlemen know
that I am a completely normal man
and pardon me if I have used vulgar language
but that is the language of the common people.

X

When my dear mother passed away
I made a firm resolution
not to allow myself to be overcome by anger
to repay insults with kindness
irony with Christian sweetness
arrogance with the humility of a lamb
no matter how shameful the provocation
although I confess that more than once I was on the point
of rebelling against the Creator
for permitting such outrages to occur.

XI

One final word:
right after God appeared to me
I took a pencil and a typewriter
and began to write down my sermons
in the best Spanish possible

not without first retiring to the desert
for a period of 7 consecutive years
without any vanity of course
even though I am illiterate
I never set foot in a school
my father was poorer than a church mouse
to put it mildly
Distinguished readers: at this moment
I am writing to you on an enormous typewriter
at a desk in a private home
no longer dressed like Christ
but like a common ordinary citizen
and I beg you very humbly
read me with a little affection
I am a man thirsting for love
and thank you very much for your kind attention.

XII
Really it makes me sad
to see people who could travel
by boat by plane whatever
die as they have lived
in the same place where they were born
always seeing the same landscape
as if they didn't have a cent
when in fact they are rolling in money
I who have traveled the whole length of Chile
without any income at my disposal
except what I earn by the sweat of my brow
I ask myself why they don't travel
is there anything in the world more interesting
especially in a country like ours
that is famous for being so beautiful
go to the nitrate works
where I worked as a young man
before my dear mother passed away
and lose yourself in the immensity of the desert
and enjoy those marvelous sunsets

believe me they look like
real aurora borealises
or visit the lake region
it's a question of picking up a public telephone
if you don't have one at home
and reserving a round-trip ticket
I can't understand why people travel so little
it must be for personal reasons
or for more important motives
and in that case it's none of my business.

XIII

Things are hopeless these days
so many people invoke the Virgin Mary
with words intended for the Father:
Our Father who art in heaven . . .
ignorance or carelessness I say
or mistakenly address the Son
as if they were talking to the Mother:
Hail Mary—full of grace
a ridiculous state of affairs
to put it mildly:
the tower of Babel fades in comparison
how the Holy Spirit must be laughing!

XIV

Minds that can only function
with sense data as their point of departure
have dreamed up a zoomorphic heaven
without a structure of its own
a simple transposition of earthly fauna
where angels and cherubim run about
as if they were barnyard fowl
completely unacceptable
I suspect that heaven resembles
a treatise in symbolic logic
more than an animal fair.

XV

"Pray for me"—some Catholics say
"I don't have time to pray
I have to go to a costume party
when I get back I'll give all of you a tip"
You have to stop those people cold
you should denounce them to the parish priest
so that he can put them in their place.

XVI

It seems clear to me
that in the long run religion and logic
are practically the same thing
you should do addition
as if you were saying an ave maría
you should pray
as if you were doing a sum
prayers and supplications yes
devilish ceremonies no
let us humble ourselves before the almighty
and stop Satan's laughter.

XVII

There are some *worthless* priests
who show up to say mass
displaying enormous artificial shadows under their eyes
and why not say it openly
with their fat cheeks and lips painted too
His Holiness should take note.

XVIII

In the centuries' old conflict
that threatens Christ's Church with another schism
I declare myself a fundamentalist:
I am in favor of mental prayer
I am the enemy of verbal prayer

even though it's none of my business
because I am a freethinker.

XIX

The priest should never laugh
what would be left for the sacristan to do
that's why I'm never tired of repeating
in manus tuas commendo spiritum meum
let thy will be done and not my own.

XX

In the real world there are no adjectives
or conjunctions or prepositions
who has ever seen an And
outside of Bello's Grammar?
in the real world there are only actions and things
a man dancing with a woman
a woman nursing her baby
a funeral—a tree—a cow
the interjection is determined by the subject
the adverb is determined by the professor
and the verb to be is a philosopher's hallucination.

XXI

I am convinced 100%
that the sexual act chills the spirit
for that reason I have remained a bachelor
in this matter I am absolutely unyielding
a priest who breaks his vow of chastity
is a sure candidate for hell
and for the same reason
I condemn with all my strength
the theory and practice of masturbation
I know of many poor depraved priests
who do it in front of a mirror
I feel sorry for them but they disgust me

if they have no self-control
they should hang up their cassocks.

XXII

Priests should learn to sing
a silent priest doesn't convince anyone
but he should pray in the style of Saint Augustine
in ecclesiastical song
individual expression is not permitted
the voice should not outshine the word
since the purpose is contact with God
and not with an artist of the vocal cords.

XXIII

And this is the challenge of the Christ of Elqui:
brave men raise your hands:
I dare you to
drink a glass of holy water
I dare you to
take communion without first making confession
I dare you to
smoke a cigarette while kneeling in prayer
you're chicken—chicken!
I dare you to
tear a page out of the bible
when the toilet paper is all gone
let's see let's see I dare you to
spit on the Chilean flag
you'd have to spit on my dead body first
I'll bet anything
that no one will laugh like me
when he is tortured by the Philistines.

XXIV

When the Spaniards came to Chile
they discovered to their surprise

that here there was no gold or silver
only lots of snow and sand: sand and snow
nothing that was worth the effort
food was scarce
and still is you will say
that is my point exactly
the Chilean people are hungry
I know that by saying these words
I can wind up in Pisagua Prison
but the incorruptible Christ of Elqui has
no other reason for living except the truth
may General Ibañez forgive me
in Chile they don't respect human rights
here there is no freedom of the press
here the multimillionaires are in control
the fox is in charge of the henhouse
of course I will ask you where
in what country human rights are respected.

XXV

All professions are really the same
there are those who say we are teachers
we are ambassadors we are tailors
and the truth is that they are priests
priests dressed or naked
priests sick or healthy
priests performing the service
even the man who cleans the sewers
is undoubtedly a priest
he more than anyone is a priest.

XXVI

To sum things up
when we take a leaf for a leaf
when we take a branch for a branch
when we confuse a forest with a forest
we are behaving frivolously

this is the essence of my doctrine
fortunately the exact shape of things
is finally becoming clear
and clouds are not really clouds
and rivers are not really rivers
and rocks are not really rocks
they are altars
             they are domes!
                    they are pillars!
and we should all be saying mass.

XXVII
Now that I've clarified things
and explained in great detail
the why the when and the how
of my personal appearance
during these 22 endless years
I hope with all my heart
that people will get the story straight
I am not a Chinaman an Arab a Mapuche Indian
that's what they said to my face
the so-called doctors of the law
when I got off the train from the north
at Mapocho Station
toward the end of 1929
I had decided to settle in the city
without suspecting that my via crucis was just beginning:
I am a son who knows what a mother means
I am a common soldier humbler than a yuyo weed
more long-suffering than the tiuque bird
more Chilean than a corn stew.

THREE POEMS

SAMUEL HAZO

LIVING'S HOW WE DIE AND VICE VERSA

Stitched with bridges, the river
   changes under crossbows
   arched at thunder, highways
   hung from steel harps,
   trestles for clocked pullmans
   and the chainlink freights.
                      The rust's
already happening.
                    Only the river
stays the same by flowing different
every different minute to the sea.
Like any follower, I read my fortune
   in the rivertow.
                 Bridging half
a century, my body changes
   while it keeps on going.
                   Resign
or rest, and what remains
   but slowing down?
                  Rely
on heaven as the nix of now,
and what's today but yesterday

plus nothing?
　　　　　　　Resist, and I
might leave some echo of myself
in blood or book before the last
assassinating clock strikes no.
The son I lucked from God
　leaves me no living to regret.
The world I make by seeing it
　and make all over just by saying
　so or writing so is all the world
　I need.
　　　　　　But seen or seen again,
it goes.
　　　　　　And, gone, it shows
that when we go, we're everywhere
at once and always nearer
for the going.
　　　　　　　Even my pipesmoke
prophesies that much of mine
or anyone's goodbye.
　　　　　　　　It twists
and dawdles through the air before
it rivers down beneath a window
sill and turns into the sky.

UNDERSTAND THE HIGHWAY, UNDERSTAND THE COUNTRY

Driving relaxes you.
　　　　　　　You like
the solitude of long trips
to nowhere in particular.
　　　　　　　Next
year you plan to drive due
north until the last road

stops in tundra—or south
as far as Tierra del Fuego.
Why?
                So you can meditate in motion.
Steering down a road, you
        study how the windshield
        frames what's coming
        while the rearview mirror
        telescopes what's gone.
                        The side
        windows smear with presences
        you can't make out until
        they're past.
                        You move against
        the earth's swivel.
                        Later, you
        sweat to put that feeling into paints
        so that your pictures move—
        move while you look at them.
No wonder you're at odds with poets.
In your beginning was the picture,
        not the word.
                        Cave paintings,
        hieroglyphics—you see them all
        as stories for the eye.
                                Television,
        film, cartoons?
                        Updated
        hieroglyphics, nothing more . . .
For you, the caravan of mile
        after mile never lies
        and never stays the same.
Driving anywhere, you're just
        a speeding witness to God's
        fresco, frame by frame: a boy
        walking a wall as if it were
        a tightrope over hell, two roofers
        shouldering a beam, an overturned
        Buick, its tires spinning

to a dead roulette.
                    You let them
memorize themselves like postcards
as you go.
          Maybe you will
read them, maybe not . . .
                              Highwaying,
you can look ahead, abreast,
behind like some twinfaced
divinity who sees in retrospect
what's coming while the past
just happens.
            Or are you King
Ulysses resurrected to repeat
a trek between the world's
absurdities and one man's
luck?
      As long as driving makes
you finally a maker of horizons,
you survive like Cain in Babylon.
The heatwave in the distance
    bends and dances in the wind
    while you roll down the windows,
    slug your will and skill behind
    the wheel and steer into the chances.

A CITY MADE SACRED BECAUSE YOUR SON'S
GRANDFATHER DIED IN IT

Your father in a wheelchair slouches
    steeply to his stroked-out side.
Your son wheels for the final
    time his final grandfather.
And you, who've walked this street
    so many times you know
    the slope and crack of every

sidewalk square, just walk
behind.
            You ask your son
(or is it just your son?)
to slow things down.
Your father flicks his good
right hand to say he can't
accept but won't deny what's
happened, that not accepting
what is unacceptable is all
life meant or means to him.
You want to hold his other
hand and squeeze it back
to life until the doctors
and their facts relent.
                The doctors
and their facts go on.
                So do
the unaffected riders in the numbered
buses.
        So does the whole
damn city that becomes no more
than just a place to live
and die in now.
            The more you walk,
the less you know the street
you knew.
            The less you know,
the more the curbs become
opposing shores.
                The street
is suddenly the river no man
steps in twice or finally outswims.
Midway between your father
and your son, you feel yourself
drawn in and on and under.

NOW

JAMES PURDY

Ken: 19
Clyde: 22

Both boys are "runaways" from small towns in Virginia and Kentucky, respectively. Ken's parents were members of an evangelical religious sect.

A flat in the East 80s, Manhattan. Broken windowpanes and green blinds. Several salvaged chairs. On the wall is an American flag found in the trash can. A few enlarged photos on the wall of famous boxers of the past, Gene Tunney, Jack Dempsey, and the German heavyweight Schmeling, left there long ago by a previous tenant. A bed which one reaches by stepladder.

Clyde enters from outside, blowing his fingers from the cold. He is poorly dressed, and his trousers are close to being in rags.

KEN. Where have you been for the past few days?
CLYDE. I just stayed home. Had a bad cold you know.
·KEN. Why didn't you phone me then?
CLYDE. Just couldn't get up the energy. (*He looks at Ken hungrily, not listening to his words but admiring Ken's anger, which makes him more handsome always.*)

KEN (*slowly, sensing Clyde's admiration*). Couldn't you have got somebody to phone me then? I sat here and waited, and waited. I even sent round to your place one night and there was no light, they said. So I decided you had run out on me.

CLYDE (*curious*): Do you imagine in your mind just how it down with these . . .

KEN (*helping him with his prevarication*). . . . bad colds . . .

CLYDE (*embarrassed by the "cue"*). . . . my bad colds, yes. (*Laughs nervously*)

KEN. So when I didn't see you for these two days, my worries began again. My worries, you know . . . over everything. (*He appeals to Clyde eloquently with reference to what troubles him.*)

CLYDE (*stung by such a question*). What? (*A bit ashamed at his question but still unwilling to hear about "worries"*) What do you worry about?

KEN. I am afraid I will lose you.

CLYDE (*in a reverie*). You do?

KEN (*also as if in a dream or alone*). I fear it. That is my daytime worry.

CLYDE. And?

KEN (*as if coming awake*). What?

CLYDE. And your other worry! (*Spoken with real passion*)

KEN (*as if "cued" by a prompter*). Oh, yes. My nighttime and other worry . . . (*Walks away from Clyde, looks out into the distance ahead of him*) I think I have gone home to see Mama. She is waiting but she is in her coffin. I know if I got into this little house of hers near the woods . . . (*He now becomes very upset and clasps his hands together.*) If I go into the little house they will put me in the same coffin they put her in! (*Turns back to Clyde*) That's my nightime worry!

CLYDE. And when do you think about me?

KEN. All the time. (*In a softer voice*) All the time. Always.

CLYDE (*musing*). And you think you'll lose me?

KEN. Sort of. . . . Yes, I'm afraid I will lose you.

CLYDE. But how could that happen, Ken.

KEN. I don't know but I fear it so.

CLYDE (*curious*). Do you imagine in your mind just how it would happen, your losing me?

KEN. No, I don't dare think.

CLYDE. But you say whether I'm with you or not you are afraid you will lose me.

KEN. That's right. That's the way it is. I keep saying to myself, *I betcha I lose Clyde.*

CLYDE (*touches Ken affectionately*). But you can count on me, Kenny. See.

KEN. I know I can, but all the while I have these bad daydreams I lose you. . . . Like I think when I'm sleeping at night I'll have to go to that lonely house in the woods and be with Mama. . . . When, Clyde, I want to be with you forever.

CLYDE. I love you, Ken. Cross my heart.

KEN. Couldn't we live together all the time like we meant it then?

CLYDE (*taken back*): Like we meant it?

KEN. Yes, like there was just the two of us in the whole world and that all we needed was to be together. . .

CLYDE (*moved*). Oh, Ken. Yes, I'd like that of course. . . . But that would be heaven. . . .

KEN. It would be *now.* That's what I'd call it if it was to be true. *Now.* It would all be now.

CLYDE. Remember the day I met you? It was raining cats and dogs. We were both living in some fleabag on 12th Avenue across the street from one another, it turned out. I saw you and then at the same time I saw this fruitstand with fresh ripe cherries. I stole a few cherries and run up to you with them. . . . *Why don't you taste a fresh spring cherry?* I said to you. You grinned and took one and ate part of it, and handed the rest to me. . . . You were the handsomest boy that day. . . . *Come home and eat the rest of them,* I said, helping myself to the whole box of fruit. *Eat them out of my hand,* I told you. . . . You came home with me. . . . I undressed you slow slow slow. . . . You didn't need to eat out of my hand though. Your lips were sweeter than any spring cherry. (*He kisses him slowly and holds him.*) Ken, I wish we could have both died right then when we were perfect together, when love was perfect. (*He begins to kiss him again, slowly, assiduously, ecstatically, very much again as if he was eating cherries.*)

KEN (*slowly extricating himself from Clyde*). Who is this man you live with, Clyde. . . . You never have told me exactly in so many words, and I've been your boy for over a year now. . . . Almost a year . . .

CLYDE. I wish we wouldn't have to talk about him.

KEN. Do you have to live with him?

CLYDE. Look, it's hard for me to hold down a steady job. . . .

KEN. So you feel you have to . . . live with him then . . . for support!!

CLYDE (*stung*). Support! Cripes! *Support.* Do you know you have just named the one thing I ain't never had. Support!

KEN (*with intense pain and a kind of bashfulness*). But don't you think, Clyde, one day . . . I mean the day might come when . . . we could live together . . . be together I mean all the time. (*Throwing himself at Clyde's knees and holding on to his legs in desperation*) I mean, Clyde, I want you all the time. . . . Not just in the afternoons like we do, understand. . . . He has you at night! This man you live with . . . That's why I have the dreams about Mama's house in the woods. He has you at night!

CLYDE (*lifting him up and kissing him*). Ken, look at me. Go on, come closer. Look at me. I look like a man, don't I. I'm big and strong. Strapping is the word. . . . Once I lifted a policeman up with one hand and threw him over a bar. . . . I can run a mile without losing my breath. I can climb a building like a fly and drop four stories without breaking a bone. . . . I can even play the harmonica! (*Whispers*) I can fuck a woman if I have to. . . . But, Ken . . . I can't earn a living! Do you hear? Do you get it? Something was left out of me when I was born. . . . That's why you and me can't live together. I can't earn! (*His voice breaks.*) I can't earn . . .

KEN (*desperate*). But supposin' I was to go out and earn a good . . . living for both of us. . . .

CLYDE (*turns away from him, weeping*). Oh, Ken . . .

KEN. I could steal. . . .

CLYDE (*bitterly*). You could, yes . . . once. . . . Then you'd be in jail. . . . No, we've got to go on the way we are. . . . I belong to him at night, and I belong to you in the day. . . . Why can't you be satisfied with that?

KEN. Because I want you at night the most, Clyde.

CLYDE. Ken, oh Kenny. (*He kisses him.*) Oh what are we going to do?

KEN. You were right about the cherries, Clyde.

CLYDE (*absent-mindedly*). Huh?

KEN. You know, when you give me the cherries you had stole, and said a little later, *I never loved anybody like this before.* We should have both died then, Clyde. . . . We were so happy those days. . . . Clyde (*Holding him*), everything else since that day has been downhill. . . .

CLYDE. Don't remind me. . . . Don't even think of it again. . . . But that was then, this is now. . . . We have to eat, Kenny, and have a place to sleep, and that's dear. . . . We got to feed ourselves and keep strong enough to see each other in the afternoon. . . .

KEN. But to go on like this, Clyde, me a dishwasher in that cheap lunchstand, and you . . . getting your support from . . .

CLYDE. Don't say anything now against Johnny. . . . Johnny's all right.

KEN. You don't love him though, do you, Clyde? . . . It would kill me if I thought you did. . . .

CLYDE. I don't love him. Not like I love you. . . . I don't love nobody like I love you. I won't ever. . . . When we ate the spring cherries together, well, Kenny, that was the end. . . . That was the end for both of us. . . . Kenny, listen, we're ghosts now. We're like old men of a hundred even! There won't never be anything that great again for us. . . . But Johnny is good. . . . He don't ask much. . . .

KEN. But he does get you at night, don't he, Clyde, tell me.

CLYDE (*hysterical*). He's not interested! It's just the warmth of another human being next to him, that's all. . . . He was in a Vietnam red prison camp, remember, and you talk about bad dreams! He don't touch me, Ken, that's gospel truth. . . . He just has to have somebody next to him at night, or . . .

KEN. Or?

CLYDE (*frightened by everything*). Well, I don't know what . . .

KEN. He wouldn't let you sleep with me one night. Just one night. I ain't ever slept with you at night, Clyde. . . . All the year I've loved you, I've been deprived of you at night. . . . I think that's why I have the bad dreams.

CLYDE. If I could do it, I would. . . . If I had the know-how and the brains to earn a living, I wouldn't stay on with him. . . .

KEN. I think you would, Clyde. . . .

CLYDE. What? (*Frightened*)

KEN. I think you would stay. . . . You love Johnny too. . . .

CLYDE. But it's not like I love you. . . . If I loved you any more I would break in two. I couldn't take any more love in my heart than you.

KEN. You love him, Clyde. . . . I'm not blaming you. . . . I see it in your face. . . . You have somebody to go home to at night. . . . And I don't have nobody. . . . I have . . . Mama. (*He says this as if he is alone.*) That's what scares me. . . . I feel . . .

CLYDE. Don't say it, Kenny. . . . Don't say it.

KEN. I will! I will!

CLYDE. Please, don't. . . . If it ain't said it won't be remembered, Kenny. Don't say it or pronounce it.

KEN. She's going to come some time and take me home. . . .

CLYDE. There now, you've said it. . . . You've hurt me, and you're glad.

KEN. Hurt *you*?

CLYDE. All right, all right. . . . I'll try to think up another way of getting by without him . . . without Johnny. (*Said in a whisper*)

KEN. But, Clyde, don't you see, if you was rich as a Arab prince you wouldn't leave Johnny. . . . Don't you know your own thoughts?

CLYDE (*as if he hadn't heard him*). I take each day as it comes, now. . . . And you're everything to me. . . . Why do we have to think beyond that, huh. . . . One day at a time, Kenny. . . . One hour, one minute at a time. (*Kisses him*) Be happy with me the way it is. . . . I'm all yours. . . . Kiss me. You've got all there is of me. . . .

KEN (*kisses but pulls away*). I want . . . more. I can't be satisfied with just days. That's not all. I want nights from you too, why can't you see that?

CLYDE. I do, Kenny, but I can't give you no more. . . . If I give you any more (*Looks into his eyes*) you wouldn't have nothing. . . . I'm givin' you all I got.

KEN. Except the nights. That's what I want so bad. . . . I want the nights with you, close against you, close against me, Clyde. . . . I want to hold you in my arms all night. Clyde, I want to be buried with you. . . . When we die, we have to leave behind a written message, instructions. . . . I want to be buried right with you. . . . I want to sleep with you forever. . . . I don't never want to be parted from you.

CLYDE (*moved*). You've brought our whole love back again, Kenny. . . . All of a sudden like it was happening for the first time.

KEN (*hardly aware Clyde has spoken*). Can't we leave that in writing? That if we should die we are to be buried together?

CLYDE. But we ain't going to die, Ken. . . . If you'll be patient, if you'll be satisfied with what there is of me, the way I am, what I have to give you. . . . If you won't want everything, Kenny! *Don't want everything*, will you?

KEN (*somewhat subdued*). I'll try. . . . But it will be hard. . . .

CLYDE (*looking out the window*). Night is coming. . . . These cold February evenings seem longer even than Christmas Eve.

KEN. Why mention it?

CLYDE (*puzzled*). What?

KEN. Christmas Eve.

CLYDE (*looking out*). The shadows are so long.

KEN. Hold me again before you go, Clyde. . . .

CLYDE (*embraces him*). You're all I've got, and all there is. (*Kisses him passionately*)

KEN. Will you write that down. . . . That in case of death, we are to be buried together. . . . Eventually . . .

CLYDE. Oh, Kenny. We're only nineteen and twenty-two. . . . You shouldn't even be thinkin' of dyin' and the tomb. It's sick to!

KEN. All right now. . . . I'm due in a few minutes anyhow at the restaurant. . . . I'm working late this week. . . . To get my mind off my blues.

CLYDE (*in reverie*). One night, Ken, my friend, you know, Johnny, had a very bad nightmare. . . .

KEN (*passionately cold*). Yeah.

CLYDE. Do you want to hear it or not.

KEN. Of course I do.

CLYDE. All right. (*Watches him hesitantly, then the story carries him along*) Johnny woke up in a sweat. . . . His sweat in fact had poured off on me so that I was wet as if I had run ten miles in the burning sun. . . . He said, and get this, *The reason I don't die is because death is in me from the war, death is sitting like he is looking at me square in the face, and has been ever since the war, the reason, then, I don't go with him and that death don't take me, is he knows I can't sleep alone yet. . . . When I learn that last lesson, then he can take me.*

KEN. That's worse than the little house in the woods with Mama! (*With passion*) It's a worse dream! . . . It's the worst. . . . It's the worst of the worst. . . .

CLYDE. What are you takin' on so bad about now, huh? (*Caresses him*) It was only his nightmare.

KEN. What do you mean, it was only his nightmare. . . . It was Johnny. . . . That was all of Johnny. . . . Like Mama and the house in the woods is all of me. . . . Don't you understand anything?

CLYDE. You're tired, Kenny. . . . And you're the youngest of us three.

KEN. I'm the oldest in dreams. . . . The oldest. . . . 'Cause I understand dreams, you hear . . . (*Softly*) I understand dreams.

CLYDE. You like Johnny a little better now. . . . I think so.

KEN. I don't like him no better because he has you at night. . . . But I can part with you maybe a little better, that's true enough.

CLYDE. That's what I guess I meant to say.

KEN (*almost as if he were alone, and again in reverie*). It's because I understand dreams, Clyde. . . . I may be just a dishwasher, never finished fifth grade, but tell me any dream anybody ever dreamed, I understand it, I'm your man.

CLYDE. And you know I love you the most, and won't never part with you. Repeat it now. . . .

KEN (*dreamily*). You love me best and won't never part with me.

CLYDE (*kisses him on the crown of his head*). Good. . . . Now so long until tomorrow, and buck up, you hear. . . . Quit thinkin' about anybody's dreams, why don't you. . . . Good-by. (*Goes*)

KEN (*alone*). The February shadows I believe are the longest and the darkest outside of what you see in dreams. . . . They lengthen and lengthen. . . . (*The stage begins to get dark as he speaks.*) But I will be satisfied I think not sleeping with him in this life if after we are dead and laid out, they will let us lie together in the grave. That will be the most happiness, for it will be forever like I want him now. It will be like when I see Mama's house and though the sun don't shine on her there, there's no end to peace and quiet, like her hand is in mine forever. That's how I'll sleep with Clyde in the sweet bye and bye. . . . (*The stage goes dark.*)

SIX FRENCH POETS

BERNARD NOËL • JEAN DAIVE • ANNE-MARIE ALBIACH •
CLAUDE ROYET-JOURNOUD • EMMANUEL HOCQUARD •
ALAIN VEINSTEIN

Selected and translated by Paul Buck

BERNARD NOËL

EXTRACTS FROM MY BODY

For Robert Maguire

. . . . .words burst level with my
skin. My eyes are fixed. My bust is a combination of movable and
immovable elements. Movements are pursued inside my chest like
rings on water. And my neck continues deep into my body. The
tree which impales my throat has sprouted and pushed from my
stomach. It climbs right into my nostrils. A short circuit cuts the
nerve currents in my nape. My head tilts towards a lake of polished
silver which suddenly disperses into space like beads of mercury.
My skull is trepanned whilst my legs are growing longer, and
longer, piercing the clouds. One side becomes painful, the other
dark. Between the two a helix revolves in my belly, the air surges

towards my mouth........ My throat is full of feathers. I spit cells..........................

The earth subsides in my body. I am the earth and the subsidence of the earth. The oesophagus is the immovable centre of this landslide. No longer is there skeleton or nerves. I see without seeing. Suffering lodges in the crevices which run across this slow collapsing—but it does not hurt.

The peritoneum cracks. I am filled with air holes. Each exertion by my eye ludicrously contracts my throat. . . . An *other* emerges in my belly without having come from outside.

Sometimes the flesh from my chest evaporates. I would like to believe it slid into my belly, but my hands refuse to find out. Or rather, I spend my time seeking my hands with a feeling of distressing urgency, as if someone was going to benefit from seeing me exposed like this. Later, with a horrifying slowness, the pleura secretes a calcareous paste which plugs up the interstices between my sides. Only then does my spine break loose along the edifice like a chimney. And it is my back that I see: a whitish mass in which saltpetre crystals are crumbling. I try to laugh about it, but nothing comes from within. The shell has emptied.

There are perceptions in nerves, skeleton, and flesh. I progress from one to the other as through bands of a spectrum. And then one perception comes to a halt throughout my body, starting with my eyes. It is this path of corpuscles crossing my bones, my flesh, scratching my nerves. More often it is like a taut fibre in a nerve fibre. That occurs particularly in my spinal cord, where everything that refers to my belly begins. The most inaccessible part of me remains my chest. The texture of my lungs. There is even, between my right armpit and my liver, a space resembling a desert. It is a sort of convex hole compared with the rest of my body. Something like the centre of coldness fitted close to the living warmth of my organs.

A chin bandage of pain. Paralysis throughout. My nose buzzes. Sudden heaviness of testicles beneath my sex. Unrest. Convolutions.

Emptiness. Emptiness. The arch of my shoulders illuminates my internal erosion. Everything flows in me as through the neck of an hourglass. No motion is thinkable: it will gel on my skin or multiply the falling sand. Emptiness. Emptiness. Flesh loess. But the traces? Where are the traces? All the unknown cannot continually dribble in me without leaving a trace. And since the whole problem now is for me to dribble in myself to cause condensation of my internal stalactite as well as to follow that trace. Of whom? Of what? What is me and the other and the *other?* My skin, certainly, and my moored organs, my nerves, my bones. The organisation. The weight of the sun holds in place the earth whose weight holds in place   My mouth does not want to be hitched right up to my anus. My eye does not want to slide into my sex. So each attempts the impossible in order to *come* independently and not to look at the emptiness   Inside, the fall continues.

That whiteness which sometimes spreads from my marrow is a weapon similar to laughter. It solidifies what could soften me. No feeling. Nothing but the rapid pulsations of transparency where my heart bleeds in fits and starts. Disencumbered of muscles, the volume is pure. The bones fall into line on my sides like silica signals. The joints have been jammed, clogged. I am bolt upright. Above, my tongue thrashes in the wind.

My mouth is that peaceable concavity surrounded by complex ways. Sealed at will, it is in itself the only hollow space by which the stranger can live in me or pass through me. It is the door to a part of my body. By contrast, my nose opens and closes a cycle of paths. I was at a loss to separate what within me depends on my mouth and what on my nose. And yet, I had forgotten it had all begun there: through the divided perception of a current of air.

Equilibrium is broken somewhere in the course of my nerves. The disorder takes over so quickly that I have already lost track of where it began. A bubble rises. There is a short circuit at my heart's peak, then the emptiness swells—an emptiness in which my suffering stomach hangs. The lower part of my stomach. The other part has flattened out beneath my shoulders. It is as if a white pyramid has inverted on my belly to impale it. My throat hardens. It becomes flaccid at uvula level, and there is a giant ebb in my whole body. A kind of panic which gathers beneath my shoulders into a sort of suffocation. In reaction, perhaps, my spinal cord becomes a luminous beam again, hypnotizing my eye.

Soft snow. Delicate snow. Snow again. And my skin flakes
through my flesh with a gentle slowness. And my flesh flakes
through my sides.
                           And
further, my vertebrae erect in the centre of my body a need
for verticality.
                           Some
ancestors pass by. Certainly, it is time which makes love
to me, and I assimilate it unendingly.
                           Where is
outside?
                           Where
is now?

My bone whitens and my face caves in on my holed skull. Nerves vibrate along edges of bones. Eyelids closed, my eye shakes its look along my marrow whilst elastic tissue lashes my liver and stomach. My teeth want to lynch my tongue. My brain wants to move out, for it is weary of my heart-pâté. My gut pants with a trembling. What terrible storm is brewing amongst my *external* organs? The space is black. My bones exude a look which strips their flesh. My eyes seek their orbits. Later, my chest is rebuilt around a current of air. Laughter again, but without laughing. And the weight of my legs clung to one another. And my blood rising once more in the remaking of my body.

My coccyx is affected before the usual waste of my look in
my belly. Suddenly my vertebrae no longer provide me with
this perfectly round canal where perception travelled
instantaneously. I locate only some peripheries, edges,
borders   always an internal subsidence, a sort
of millenary crater   and everywhere
an endless fall, a fall around which my organs live or
survive, packaged by my skin   Nothing
but a residue, from which my body can always restart, or
be destroyed   But I am afraid.
I smoke from habit. I repaint my skin. I put women into my
eye   Continual woman or new woman, one to

anaesthetize the sensation of the fall, the other to provoke
that expiration which is the rise of emptiness into my
throat   and the hope of the sputum   of the
liberating sputum   Nevertheless,
it is not a question of expelling the emptiness, but of
crossing it *in my body.*

In the beginning, my eye visited my marrow, and I was born. My
sex emerged opposite my eye to look at the time, and slowly my
marrow span a ball of nerves around which the hours drained. This
was my belly. The water was then thirst to be seized, and it con-
densed my skin. The softness begat its contrary, and my bone ap-
peared. There was an inside and there was an outside, but the
inside contained its own outside which said *me* whilst it said *i*. My
eye expelled them into the dark and turned towards the outside
outside. I had a face, a volume, a body. I was a plenum which
forged ahead. But here my eye has inverted. Now, I see behind.
Now I am hollow and my body is ready to begin again.

1956

AH . . .

ah . . . not screamed, sputtered, repeapeated, ah-ah-ah, squeezed between teeth, hardly need the obsolete tongue, languifying the vivid, licking the read, ah . . . stunned that it can make no more than this ah, and forcing, panting, pushing, pumping, my head empty all around, buzzing and empty, emptying only emptiness into my mouth, where the ahahing swells with impatience, going at it again with an ah-ah-ah to make its tip rise and tap the back of my palate, and, nothing, finding nothing, touching nothing, eventually flopping, flabby tonglut, meaty and limp, bestial, drifting aimlessly in saliva, but soon risen again, off again, ah-ah, ah-ah, with a burst that hurls it into my eye socket where its effort snares it, hanging there like a rag at half-mast, peltified, pleated, panting enough to cause a current of air in deserted heights and shake: a, b, d, e, r, n, e, l, n, o, r, the final letters of its alphabet, whose dust flies, then falls, blending its remains with the remains of the swallowing and preparing a soft mud of the last wash ou . . .

ah . . . after me: aaaaah . . . and nothing is more like a tongue than another, though each wants to prevent the others from tonguing around . . . aaaaah how they are still drawn out, listening to it . . . ah what a tongue . . . listening to them linked, listening to the glibness, and marking time, an immobile hour, so they can unendingly say its happiness, sadness and whatever can be said with word permutations, while, empty teats, empty phalli, they swell with blood, sperm, and the dream of its words, ah starving themselves of themselves through it, and so taken with the game of being what they are not, thus raised, they no longer look like what they are, but like those long lines one sees in old cemeteries, where, at the head of each grave, the earth sticks out a stone tongue on which one can make out the remnants of alphabets, in hollows traced as if with some stick in the dust . . .

ah . . . flowing . . . ah, as if carried away by the birth fluid, and in that water rolling, rolling, aaaaah far from the bony belly which is my head, which, in front, has a slit whence pokes my tongue, fucking words between teeth, fucking, not by intromission but by hit-and-run, out-in, out-in, inverting the virile movement, since it ousts what is housed and ends by rehousing, without one knowing though, whether, back in the mouth, the tongue simply continues to make saliva or whether it gives this cunt a cock and a completion in an androgyny, proof that, once the signified is expelled, all is sexualised within to knot letter to letter, striking work . . .

1977

Jean Daive

IMAGINARY WHO FOR B.N.
AND 12 RADIO STATIONS (extract)

in the head-sky
my shadow
            is the shadow
of my last coin.

i've led a pack of habits

The bewildered dispensation: any resemblance
re-sold, hired out or otherwise exchanged.

i don't want the expiation of Oedipus

To mimic, to mill the family quota:
a distribution as temporal reading of us.

someone consumes his look
        consumes the currency of the narrative.

devoured   devouring

Land reserves.

whoever would like to mint money from the absolute
would count only the faces of the wind

        Who civic, rural, urban, whole—the dog of the
        world barks throughout the century, reproduces
the look of the narrative.

hunger from being hungry

Hunger from applying the example, the figure
of the example.

in the past we chewed over knowledge
to give a name to each thing

Emission of a reality always contrary:
remains only to name, to erase, to add
nothing.

the blue of the real
delayed our hunger

Forever as ever, a grammarian intimacy.
Currency whose tongue holds back the
hand, me beneath thing, beneath sleep.

There's no beginning again. There is
periphrasis. Of the man who tells his
story and of the silver which causes
the dream the night before. I remem-
ber. You were listening to me. Every-
one recognised us. We are tiny totality
subjected to the volume in which we
disappear. Madam, three leopards lull
my child. Everything becomes spaced
out in the light of the dawn. To speak
burns. We protect ourselves from the
utterable word by making it implode
in its fiction. How to reveal? Can the
inevitable be revealed? This: I attain
the memory soaked with cracks which
promises to be the proper place for
the interrogation of the one whose
speech turns round in the resemblance.
Between no and no. Between nothing
and no. Between abyss and no. Mod-
estly and preceded. Always. The neu-
ter as nothing. Then a first stair. And
the flight of. To enter, to become that
passable space ascribes to us the role
of a descent into hell. We earn what
we consume. To descend. To descend.
Through the movable shadow. Be-
cause the leaf is unscathed, Madam, I
sell the foliage of all the first times to
the sugar tombs. Descending the stair-
case of nothing. Towards you. Who
looks at me and wears a long veil, a
sea. Where I descend. We are speak-
ing to each other, aren't we, tongue
to tongue, from one sea to the other.
Two apprentices. But you know. You
who have made me visible by italics.
And I lose you as I place on my
speech, on our speech, my reading

time. My time full stop. I want you
again. Beneath me, beneath my legs.
I am a presentiment of you. I am the
time of an ungraspable proximity. I
am a real grammarian. I am a thing
which is simply impersonal and which
speaks and which communicates in all
like ways or not. I am far from you. I
no longer hear. I no longer hear you.
Who? But we are, aren't we? We are
filled with words of every sentence.
We are marvellously alike. We hire
out our resemblance, our time. But as
all resounds and becomes and comes
back. You speak. You pass. Nothing
sinks in the red anymore. Hair col-
oured ash-grey with nothing. To
speak. I speak. That's to say. I receive
the dividend of the added thing.
Don't understand value. In sum, thing
as measure and me as proposition.
Twisted sentences. I associate tongue
and bank. I associate me and cotton-
stalks. In the morning, I make a read-
ing of my sentence: I turn the stalk
in my ear. How should I say it? Do
you understand? That sentence which.
Since the head. Twirls. Around cot-
ton. In the ear. And is written. The
words are always missing, but we ac-
company them. After what should one
write? And why? Standing in a li-
brary, I discovered Can you imagine
Hegel naked between the legs of a
woman, and his mouth full of shit?
But can you imagine Hegel, similarly
naked, and like an Algerian, pissed on
by parachutists? Before speaking it is
necessary to choose one's likeness.

Perhaps. We are in the same. We speak to the same. "He" has lost his side. "He" works above from the infinity. "He" counts his money. "He" advances. Me, I advance. I talk to myself. Roses in my hair. I am in jeans and I am the bride. I must revive myself. I must hold on. Because everything is expressed, I wanted to see the speech of the Other opening to the dream like a woman who is sleeping, a sea of cushions between her arms and speaking in her dream into the pillow where I am. Speech, war and cloud. Still. To glide. To drift. But I foresee the passage of speech in the murder. I speak because I am dead. I speak because I want to reply to words. Because I want to reply with words. To be simply invisible through what the mouth thinks. In the middle of the sea, I am. With the immense displacement. Pigs from every country and vegetables, counters, commercial land, monetary exchange that I cross. I read walking on the sea. The sea. My judicial advance.

ANNE-MARIE ALBIACH

"DISCOURSE"

1

where TWO
          is inverted in the field
oblation of a memory BODY of nine words

In an obtuse manner
language runs into that partition
walking
          so as   mobile
     cited
nine : the intervention of the multiple breach
     "that"
named throughout the line
     a cube
attains its generation
of verbs in three supple tenses

          "to a good day"
gave the sign which broke the cube
               (thus will they go out to the waiting which unseals
               murky darknesses where stammering signifies terror)

THEME

If coldness reaches the body

pose: a slowness

    in the interruption
Objects: "at each movement"

mimesis,

        the dazzling

RESPIRATION

        the breath
            hides a gloomy accusation

        the body unfolds

Objects

    the designation

        : following the outline

of the image,

*"outside the gratuity
of a taken position"*

the song:

of *blue* encircled

in proportion to the obscure
in the desire

the gesture gradually

could free the passage

in the close light

OF THE VOICE

the ring around the wrist

in the declination

: an alternation appears *from black to white*

the multiple degrees

in *excess*

instability of the support: a cavity in the reflection;

In the intervention
like the duality of the course

still she, brought back to her gesture

musical

"linear flesh

*a belt at the bend
in the centre
oscillation"*

burnt back

the arachnidan doors

: THE CUP

failing the hand

"of the blade and the sore of the tissue"

he would carry an offering

Into the confined space

the porticoes

the liquidity of the i

Claude Royet-Journoud

VOICE IN THE MASK

the achievement of this task
opens onto sleep

*as this body
in its loss
takes on sense*

a force passes from hand to hand

to bring everything back to black

*vicious tongue
threadbare*

it knows only its walls

fiction
by fits and starts

TIE-BEAM

she incites the fall and the breaking up

the pain lodges in the left wrist

look at him
he has no tongue!

an abandoned sentence
it's from there they started

    into the simulacrum
        the nutritious exterior

"and the wild beasts that wander the mountains"

it's at the edge of a sentence
        of a terror without object

they are set in motion
they penetrate the ground

behind the image

to come to its description

he takes the book again
a pile of stones

dead tongue
around the mouth

Emmanuel Hocquard

YOU THIS PLACE
ALSO VERY WHITE: THE BRANCHES

The clouds. You distant, you the mouth. The space more
at the edge. Here we are away from usual courses.
Assigned to the day.

It's morning. You know the shadow which forms.

From one place to the other the passage: a door on
the water. Fine weather, all around, as far as the
eye can see over the trees.

The silting of the river. The echo. The flowers. Blue
in vain that the name throws back to the silence.

Airsplits, your statues.

Speaking. Well into the night, the tables. What could
be held over to the next day: the linen folded in the
sun, the nettles on the footpath.

Now the history is known. You via fragments of events
and strange circumstances.

A game improvised during the storm, on the opposite
side of the horizon.

ALAIN VEINSTEIN

SAME SCENE

Nothing.   Elements of space,
last remains of the child, yes,
what child?
Since the death I've decided,
it's written, totally, all—
to forget the scene
I've decided to the point of no longer being—
all she, it's, always loved, written
what happens to a man, no
what can happen:
when I'm afraid I write, I write
what catches my breath—
After the emergence of the words the end
I write so that nothing comes through.

Longing to flee. I can't flee
the cries of a child's voice
collapsed in my arms.
I stop. I wait for the words the end.
I'm stopped, having all the words
to find the words the end.

Despite its force—pain—
without restraint, in front of—
a sharp gesture, hatred, not a word,
not had a word—as
coldly death—
coldly—despite its force—

hatred—
greedy, each time, to rebegin—
I pass, each time, to the moment of the scene—
to pound, beat,
leave me wordless.

Already there.   Same scene.   Through
desire to write, I've recalled it, that night,
and today, it's real, always above there is
pain, there is, coldly,
like the knife. I'd written it.
Same place. I resume.
It's strange I resume
after the repetition of blows,
but nothing let be foreseen then
the course of the history:
there were blows, pains,
much hurt that did not emerge.

I hadn't wanted it—
nothing changed—it's hardly as if—
the first blow doesn't break the silence
(a great big word silence
when one hasn't entered)—
then blows, blows,
not a crime, everyday life . . .
Nothing buried here—
blows don't make a drama—
but try as I might to keep to the surface,
I write with words that hold back the terror.

NOTES ON THE POETS AND TRANSLATOR

ANNE-MARIE ALBIACH was born in 1937. While living in London in the 1960s, she edited *Siècle à Mains* with Royet-Journoud and Michel Couturier. Her first book was *Flammigère* (Siècle à Mains, 1967). Her second, *État* (Mercure de France, 1971) attracted much attention. Translated extracts have appeared in *Modern Poetry in Translation* and *The Literary Supplement* (both U.K.). For a period she only published *"H II" lineaires* (Le Collet de Buffle, 1974). Recently her work has appeared in diverse publications: *Diagraphe, Change, Première Livraison, Exit, Terriers, Action Poétique, Critique, Argile* (translated here), *Orange Export Ltd.*

PAUL BUCK was born in 1946. Of his many books of poetry and prose, his main ones are: *Pimot* (Latimer Press, 1968), *re/qui/re(qui)re* (Pressed Curtains, 1975), *Lust* (Pressed Curtains, 1976), and *Violations* (Pressed Curtains, 1979). He is currently editing five hundred pages of his notebook *fou:tr:et* for publication, and finalising volume two of his ten-volume prose project *Lust*. He has edited *Curtains* since 1971, presenting over forty contemporary French writers alongside English and American poets. As a result of censorship of his projects, he has recently moved *Curtains* to a Paris base. He has translated many French writers but is particularly interested in Bataille, Noël and Faye. He recently co-edited an *Anthology of New English Poetry*, to be published in Paris in a bilingual edition in 1980 by Christian Bourgois. In gathering the material for "Six French Poets," he would like to thank Claude Royet-Journoud, François de Laroque, and Glenda George for their counsel.

JEAN DAIVE was born in 1941. His earlier work was published in *L'Éphémère*, and later in *Fragment*, a magazine he founded in 1970. His first book, *Décimale blanche* (Mercure de France, 1967) was published in translation as an edition of *Origin* by Cid Corman in 1969. In recent years a number of books have appeared, including *Fut bâti* (Gallimard, 1973), *Le Jeu des séries scéniques* (Flammarion, 1976), *1, 2, de la série non aperçue* (Flammarion, 1976), and *Le cri-cerveau* (Gallimard, 1978). Other translations have appeared in *Curtains* (U.K.), *Modern Poetry in Translation, Square One* (U.K.). He is the youngest contributor to C. A. Hackett's *New French Poetry* (Blackwell, 1973). This text is taken from *Givre 2/3*, devoted to Bernard Noël.

EMMANUEL HOCQUARD has published three booklets with Orange Export Ltd., the press that he runs with the artist Raquel: *Le Portefeuil, Les Espions Thraces Dormaient Près Des Vaisseaux*, and *Toi Ce Lieu Très Blanc Aussi: Les Branches* (translated here). *Album d'images de la Villa Harris* (Hachette, 1978) helped to launch a new collection directed by Paul Otchakovsky-Laurens. *Les Dernières Nouvelles de l'Expédition* (Hachette, 1979) has subsequently appeared.

CLAUDE ROYET-JOURNOUD was born in Lyon, France, in 1941. While living in London in 1963, he founded the review *Siècle à Mains*, with co-editors Anne-Marie Albiach and Michel Couturier. He now lives in Paris. Translations of his poems have appeared in *Doones, Curtains* (U.K.). and *Modern Poetry in Translation*. His first collection of poems, *Le Renversement* (1972), was published by Gallimard and translated as *Reversal* by Keith Waldrop (Hellcoal Press, 1973). The poems here are taken from his second Gallimard collection, *La notion d'obstacle* (1978).

BERNARD NOËL was born in 1930. After publishing *Extraits du corps* (Minuit, 1958) (first section translated here), he stopped writing and did not reappear until the late 60s. From that time onwards he has published a number of volumes of poetry, collected up to 1970 as *Extraits du corps* (10/18, 1976), as well as three novels, *Le Château de Cène* (Pauvert, 1971), *Les Premiers Mots* (Flammarion, 1973), and *Le 19 octobre 1977* (Flammarion, 1979), all of which have attracted much attention, the first as the subject of a court case for *outrage aux moeurs*. Equally he is known as a perceptive essayist and editor, recent contributions being *Treize cases du je* (Flammarion, 1975), and *Magritte* (Flammarion, 1976). He has been awarded a number of prizes, and is regarded as the natural successor to Georges Bataille and Maurice Blanchot. His work has been appearing in translation in English magazines, particularly *Curtains*, and in America in *Invisible City* and *Substance*. An issue of *Spectacular Diseases* (Peterborough, England) was recently devoted to his work. Translations of his novels, récits, and poetry are in progress by Paul Buck and Glenda George.

ALAIN VEINSTEIN was born in 1942. His earlier work was published in magazines like *Mercure de France, L'Éphémère,* and *Fragment,* while his later work appears in *Argile* (from which his poem here is translated), *Clivage, Action Poétique, Première Livraison,* and *Orange Export Ltd.* He has published *Répétition sur les amas* (Mercure de France, 1974), *Qui l'emportera?* (Le Collet de Buffle, 1974), *Recherche des Dispositions Anciennes* (Maeght, 1977), and *Vers l'absence de soutien* Gallimard, 1978). Two long poems have been translated in *Modern Poetry in Translation* and *Curtains*, (U.K.).

THREE POEMS

MARK RUDMAN

HOMECOMING

Another grim November,
no way out of that.
I was under the same
hard thin layer of cloud
all day. It will stretch,
a friend said in Setauket,
to February. Then I saw
the tarpaulin strung.

An endless field
matted down by weeks of rain.
The bruised earth:
it cringes under our footsteps.
We walk on.
I pick up mud from one spot
and drag it to another.
Stray clods of dirt harden.

The shadowed underbelly of a plane,
wind, rain,
let the elements change.

The train windows, as always, are bleared,
like the voluminous cloud that shadows everyone,
now, as the season takes over,
forests razed, wood stacked,
flues opened,
the animals let in,
the rooms, as always, filling with stray things,
posters from exhibitions that have gone away hung on the walls,
whatever enters now, will stay.

DEER ISLE AND VOICES

Beginning, not with our
arrival in the night
but with our first morning walk to the dock in the rain
and the gull who, stunned out of sleep
deep in heaps of net
piled on net, rises drowsily, and angles off,
if this is possible,
without beating his wings,
which brings me back
to the rain
and only through the slight
prickling sound it leaves
on the thick
transparent plastic tarpaulin
can we hear it at all,
knocked out by the stalwart mortarless
stone foundations in Maine
homes on the shoreline;
it is the ease with which they
receive the slashing
wave that imparts
loveliness to them.

My neighbor swears
the fireworks will be

worth seeing, and says
it's o.k. to stand
on the slippery dock
so long as you hold
onto the rail.

The fireworks do a fine
imitation of the
constellations,
ghost voices drift
over the water,
rippling under hulls,
scored rock,
incisions, wounds,
the boats that turn and turn
at anchor and spray shadows
everywhere,
turning, I see
tiers of houses
slanted on cliffs,
river, rivulet, and ditch,
luminous,
kids swinging sparklers in the dark
like censers,
lanterns hung
from the one beam
that will flood
the porch with light,
caracole
over two dwarf pines
rooted in shallow sand,
and bodies huddled
around a toy
cannon appear,
faintly present
in the red light under the flares.

Distraction sets in. Gossip
of lobstermen. I overhear them
talk of the warden, fall guy

for the decline in the numbers
they haul out of the deeps,
the abandoning of the quarry
counts for nothing,
and they assail the warden
wonderfully,
"who sits on this
green schooner cut trim
as any canoe, the one
whose sails are never hoisted,
smoking cigars and drinking Martinis . . .
and when he caught me out there hauling
freezing my ass in the late November dark
I thought sure he'd revoke my license flat,
that sonofabitch, hell, it isn't fair,
there are guys out there without licenses,
raking out our traps in the dark
who don't care if they get caught—
but lobstering's the only thing I know."

SALVAGING

1

Light from the hallway seeps under the door.
I wear the night over my eye like a patch.

I lock the doors. The walls close in.
The glaciers holler. I can't hear them.

What's conceived is barely spoken.
If it gets too dim, call it mist.

I pawned my brain in order to be reasonable.
The claim ticket's misplaced, not lost.
Inside the old house, thick with musk,
the walls of the matriarch are lined with mink.

2
I arrive at the station. The train is empty,
but cannot accommodate any more passengers.

Snow covers the tracks. A white animal pauses.
I touch my beard and my hand fills with snow.

The child hugs the doll, the doll hugs her back;
the child dies of shock and they bury the doll.

The matador pauses before the kill:
there is more to this flourish than show.

Choices bleed into acts: you sit at ringside,
but are no spectator, unless you can keep dry.

3
The perilous instant is blessed: witness the ant
scaling crevices on the butcher-block counter.

Another seasonal shift: a pigeon's trapped
in the airshaft. Continual threat of avalanche.

I keep glancing at the calendar on my watch
wondering why it is so cold if it is nearly spring.

I hear the prisoners were asked to redesign the fortress
for the prevention of suicide in the death cell.

Clusters of galaxies in my coffee cup. One long sip and the rims
are smeared with the flotsam of exhausted stars.

4
No news to report, but yesterday a crack in the
sky became a scar on the cheek of heaven.

I do not believe in omens and yet my heart leapt at the sight

of an opossum in a death trancing baring his pearly fangs at
the moon.

The simple life eludes me: the autumn sky inside my head
is a sheet of lead, angelic and sinister.

Nightly I watch the same promiscuous commercial in muggy color.
My head throbs. One mistake and a life lost in the making.

To what can the spirit adhere? Old shoes with dirt sticking
to the soles: more simple things to blind us into saying yes.

5
On either side of the road there is danger: nameless beasts
that make strange moans and never show their faces.

I don't need you anymore to tell me which turn to take.
I can stomach pain; it is deceit that undoes me.

I know I have built my house with the bricks of anxiety
but to feel nothing hurts most in the long run. The long run.

The men that thought franchise was ownership left us hanging
upside down and went away singing the songs we taught them.

Five birds wing it out of one nest the size of a saucer.
And still they cart the night away in phosphorescent trucks.

6
I love this sodden landscape where tree, telephone,
and plumbing combine to make a vast network of pulsations.

The aspects of pain I can live without, like frost
on a frozen leaf, are superfluous.

The fog is an unformed face, embryo of unknown
species that come and go with the weather.

The weather survives the weather: wingless, eye-
less, tongueless, it can't remember to forget.

The arena is empty: it is time for the spectators to die.
One instant of silence is louder than history's accumulated noise.

HISTORY IS ON OUR SIDE

VILAS SARANG

Translated from the Marathi by the author in collaboration with Breon Mitchell

Study your palm when you wake up in the morning: that's a well-known Sanskrit saying. One has to admit that the young people of today may not be familiar with it. What do you read in your palm, they might ask. It is pointless to answer such questions. What can those who have no strength in their arms see in their palms?

As always, I woke at five. I inspected the palm of my right hand. The life line is very strong indeed, I said to myself. God be praised.

I rose from the bed and approached the calendar on the wall. The corner laundry gives away calendars to its customers each year before Christmas. As a matter of fact, I usually wash my clothes at home. But every year, a few days before Christmas, I take my two woolen jackets to the laundry, and make it a point to ask for a calendar when I collect them. I like to have this particular calendar, because it shows each date on a separate slip. Each day you tear off a date. Such calendars are not popular anymore, but I prefer this type to the calendars common now. Tearing off a date daily is an excellent way of reminding yourself of the passing of time. It is like handing Him a receipt for each day you've been blessed with. I prefer acknowledging receipt promptly in this way, instead of doing so at the end of a month, or even of two or three months. The large stock of slips that one sees in January diminishes gradually. The other day I thought: little by little one cuts away this cancerous knot, and yet it reappears obstinately each year! Such bizarre notions often come into my head nowadays.

I went to the calendar and tore off the date. With the torn slip wadded up in my fist, I stared at the new date.

June 11. Today I am seventy, I said to myself.

I went to the door to throw away the ball of paper, but, forgetting to do so, I stood in the doorway pursuing a train of thought. I remembered that in my childhood my birthday used to be a holiday, for it was also the birthday of King George V. He is no longer on the throne, his successors have left this country, and I cannot take childish delight in my holiday birthday anymore. Another thought that occurred to me was that according to the Bible, a man's lifespan is seventy years, whereas our Hindu faith considers it as a hundred years. I have reached seventy, God be praised. Now, if I am to live to be a hundred, how am I going to spend another thirty years?

At this point I realized I was crushing the wad of paper in my fist. I flung it outside, and gripped the doorframe with both hands. A number of incoherent questions crossed my mind. What has this doorframe got to do with my being seventy? What is my relationship to persons born seventy years ago and no longer living? What proof exists, except a few pieces of paper, that I have lived for seventy years? Should I buy a new pair of sandals for my birthday? Or would I prefer a pair of fancy cufflinks?

I decided that finding solutions to these questions would take a considerable amount of time, and therefore turned from the doorway and occupied myself with my daily chores. I had decided upon one thing: I wished to spend this day like any other day. Except in one respect—I intended to devote more time to contemplation than I usually did.

Squatting over the basin in the lavatory, I found myself still thinking over the questions that had assailed my mind. After relieving myself, it is my custom to study the stool, although it is admittedly somewhat difficult to do so in a squatting posture. Also, one might wonder what benefit accrues from the exercise. Does one expect to have disburdened oneself of rocks or stones, or to have been relieved of gold and diamonds? All that one ends up observing are slight changes in color and firmness. Sometimes there are tiny worms, or, if a hemorrhoid has bled, bright little red banners. Profitless though it may be, my habit persists. On this occasion, however, my mind was so preoccupied with the questions besetting it that the faeces slid down the drain before I thought of peering down. Not that this mattered much. And yet I was somewhat upset.

Before setting out for a morning walk, I slipped a slice of guava into the parrot's cage. When he saw me leaving the house, he screamed as usual: "History is on our side." This is the only sentence the parrot can speak. Whenever I go out, or return, or when someone comes to visit, or leaves, he shouts this message. With these confident words ringing in my ears, I stepped out.

The morning breeze was exhilarating. The nights had been unduly warm. I noticed a few clouds in the sky. The monsoon was almost upon us. I'm going to see yet another season of rain, I said to myself. In recent years, I had watched monsoon showers mostly through the horizontal iron bars of my windows.

As usual I went to the Mahatma Gandhi Garden. I sat upon a bench.

The sun was rising. Small birds chattered.

I rose and turned home.

Nearing my house, I found that the roadmen had arrived with barrels of asphalt, heaps of gravel, a steamroller, and other paraphernalia of their trade. They had put up a sign in the middle of the road: ROAD CLOSED, UNDER CONSTRUCTION.

It appeared that the municipality was intent upon repairing the roads before the onset of the monsoon. Then traffic would flow smoothly. Automobile drivers would not curse the municipality, pedestrians would not curse automobile drivers for spraying them with muddy water, and bier-carriers would not curse the dead. I went into my house.

At half past nine I heard a knock upon the door. I was a little surprised, for I didn't expect anyone. (I seldom expected anyone, for that matter.) I opened the door. It was a man, about fifty, and his face seemed familiar. Then I remembered: it was Sadanand Karkare. It was quite a surprise. I hadn't seen Sadanand for twenty years or so. He used to be a thin young man, but now he looked plump.

I was nearing fifty back then. Sadanand was one of my rare history major students. In the smalltown college where I taught, few students got to the stage of specializing for the bachelor's degree, and fewer still majored in history. Sadanand turned out to be an intelligent man. We used to talk for hours, and he helped me with my research on several occasions. He often remarked that he wanted to remain single and devote himself to research, following my example. I warned him that it was an arduous, austere life. Then he graduated, and went to another town as a schoolteacher. Both of us were sorry to part. A few months later I received a wedding card from him, and then a letter; I didn't write back. Two or three years later someone informed me that Sadanand's wife had died during her first pregnancy. Then for years I had no news of him. And now he stood in front of me, holding his baggage.

Sadanand put his bags down, and wiped the sweat off his brow. He sat in the chair to which I pointed. "History is on our side," the parrot screamed. Sadanand gave a start.

Sadanand stared at me. I observed him. Twenty years ago his face looked somewhat boyish and delicate. Now, at fifty, the face had withered, and yet it carried a suggestion of the dew of youth, or so I fancied. He said: "I've been teaching school all these years. I'm not tied down, but I've never been able to do the research I wanted to. And I wanted to see you, or at least to write, but I didn't. I was eager to see your study on the battle of Kurukshetra. When it came out, I read it again and again. Now I too have started on a piece of research. I felt I needed your advice. Finally, I decided to come down. I knew today was your seventieth birthday, and I thought it offered a good occasion to see you after so many years. Congratulations!"

Sadanand opened a box of candy, and held it out to me. As a rule I refrain from eating between meals. Also, I avoid sweets, and prefer foods that have a bitter or astringent taste, which help the system to avoid ills like biliousness. But on this occasion, I did not have the heart to refuse the gift that Sadanand, whom I was seeing after so many years, was offering with such affection. So as not to hurt him, I selected a piece of candy.

"I was captivated by your book on the battle of Kurukshetra," Sadanand said. "Approaches to the writing of history have become etxremely hackneyed. I believe you have successfully broken new ground, and developed new techniques."

The story of my book on the Kurukshetra battle is this: I set out to write an account of the battle, but the fact that the battle between the Moguls and the Peshwas was fought at the same site centuries later kept intruding into my thoughts.* Things became more complicated when I found details of the Arab-Israeli wars, the India-Pakistan wars, and the Vietnam war getting mixed up in my mind with the Kurukshetra battle. My book finally took the shape of an unusual amalgam of these different wars. I had the book published in Poona by investing part of my savings. I knew that historians would fail to see the significance of my method. As I expected, there were few reviews, and those that appeared were virulently denunciatory.

"What fascinated me was your technique of telescoping different wars," Sadanand said. "It should open totally new vistas in the field of historical writing."

"I didn't exactly invent what you have called the technique of telescoping," I explained. "It just happened that way. I cannot claim much credit for it."

"You say that out of modesty, sir," Sadanand maintained. "But what distresses me is that so-called historians should so criminally ignore the breakthrough you have made."

I didn't say anything.

Sadanand said, "Now let me turn to my own ideas, however poor they might appear in comparison to your magnificent insights. I have come to believe that traditional methods of writing history, such as studying documents and ancient inscriptions, are in the final analysis inadequate. The question is, can we arrive at the true nature of historical personalities by such methods? Perhaps there are things in their life that never get into documents or inscriptions. It is my opinion that we must focus our attention upon these other things, hidden in the darkness of the unspoken. Convinced of this, I have now embarked upon a biography of the emperor Chandragupta. I have completely ignored what are called, with charming naïveté, primary sources. I sit down with nothing but blank paper before me, and write."

I said, "I sincerely wish you success in your experiment. If young men like you began to display such an intrepid spirit, I am sure historiography will witness a renaissance. I only hope that I shall still be in this world to see your work on Chandragupta completed."

* The battle of Kurukshetra, fought between the Pandavas and the Kauravas, is the subject of the *Mahabharata*. It is more legend than history.—V. S.

"Please don't say things like that," Sadanand said quickly. "I'm sure you will live for many more years. With your blessings I hope to complete my project, and to dedicate the monograph to you."

I have to admit that I was rather touched. It seemed to me that the seventy years of my life had not been altogether wasted.

Sadanand rose from his chair, and went towards the parrot's cage. The parrot leered at him with one eye, and then screamed, "History is on our side." Sadanand turned and walked to the window by the door. He gazed outside. One could hear the rumbling of the steamroller outside, and the voices of the laborers. I watched Sadanand.

Then Sadanand unpacked his bags. He lifted a large box and placed it on my desk. "Look," he said. "A tape recorder." I was somewhat surprised. How could a mere schoolteacher afford to buy a tape recorder? Sadanand seemed to discern my thoughts. "I invested much of my savings in this," he said. "Another of my plans is now materializing. The idea is to record the silence of historical places. It occurred to me that people only take pictures of historical places. How much can we learn from pictures alone? Auditory reality is important too. So I decided to visit various historical sites and record the silence there. Naturally, the silences are perforated by background noises. For instance, my recording at the Red Fort in Delhi caught the tourist guide's commentary; luckily, one can't make out what he is saying. The recording in front of the Taj Mahal picked up the sound of a small stone a boy threw into the water. In the caves on Elephanta Island near Bombay there was the screeching of a solitary monkey. However much you try to keep out sounds, they intrude. But if you listen carefully, you will hear the silence behind the sounds. I haven't been able to travel about a great deal. How can one afford it on a schoolteacher's salary? Now that I'm here, I'd like to record the silence in the Mogul tomb outside town."

Then Sadanand played his tapes for me, and the silence of ancient places held me in thrall.

At lunch Sadanand reminisced over our days together, but I noted that he avoided talking about his marriage. The piece of candy that I had eaten that morning had taken away my appetite. My stomach cannot digest sweets easily. I ate a little lunch merely to keep Sadanand company.

After lunch Sadanand went out with the tape recorder. I lay down for a siesta, but was unable to sleep. I listened to the steamroller thundering outside in the afternoon silence.

After a while I felt a need to relieve myself. This was unusual, for I am extremely regular in my habits. I seldom have a bowel movement except early in the morning. I assumed that the candy I ate in the morning was responsible for the present situation. My body was in a hurry to purge itself of a substance that was not agreeable to it. I felt it was a mistake to have eaten it. Yet, nothing was gravely amiss. All would be well after a satisfactory evacuation.

I went to the lavatory. I stepped in, and saw a lizard on the wall, close to the ceiling. I stood still.

This was not the first time that I had seen a lizard on the lavatory wall. There is a small attic above the lavatory, and the ventilator at the back extends to the attic. So the lizards in the attic often slip into the lavatory in search of insects, especially at night.

I have a horror of lizards, and killing them is not easy. A blow with the broom is not really effective. Usually only the lizard's tail remains in front of you, twitching in a maddening manner.

What offends me particularly, however, is the sight of a lizard in the lavatory. I have found a way of exterminating them. With a raised broom, I slowly get as close to the lizard as possible. The lizard regards me with beady eyes, ready to streak away instantly. Deftly I give it a lightning blow. It usually falls to the floor, knocked out momentarily, but not yet dead. Quickly I shove it into the lavatory basin, and immediately pull the chain. Before it has had a chance to come to, the lizard vanishes down the drain. The strategy demands special dexterity at two points. First, when the lizard falls to the floor, you must toss it accurately into the basin. If you miss, it will regain its senses and get away before you have a second chance. Secondly, you have to pull the chain quickly, or the lizard may climb out before the water flushes it down. If all goes well, it is an extremely effective way of eliminating lizards.

Now, too, I advanced towards the lizard with a broom in my hand. I struck, the lizard fell, and I hastily tossed it towards the basin. I missed, however, and the lizard landed on the other side of the basin. Before I could strike again, it had climbed up the wall, reached the ventilator, and disappeared into the attic.

I went and put away the broom. If I had killed the lizard, I would have sat down to relieve myself with a sense of satisfaction. Nevertheless, it was all right to sit down now, for there was little likelihood that the lizard would descend again soon. I squatted, but without success. I was annoyed, for this had seldom happened. Many years ago I suffered from hemorrhoids, but I have never had to submit to the miseries of constipation. I wondered if the candy I had eaten was causing all this trouble, or if it was due to the disquiet generated by my failure to dispatch the lizard. I came out of the lavatory. I paced about.

There was a knock on the door. Sadanand came in, put his tape recorder down on the desk, and announced, "For once I was able to record pure silence." He played the tape. I could hear the faint but sharp sound of a "nightbug," a cicada. "Oh, I didn't even notice that there was a nightbug chirping," Sadanand said. If it chirps at midday, why does one call it a nightbug, I wondered.

It occurred to me that Sadanand's return had made me feel better. I had lived alone for many years; I did not need anyone. I do not mean the kind of thing one refers to when one says, for instance, that one needs a servant. I mean a terrifying need from which a man must do his best to keep his distance. I have seen people possessed by this need, and have seen what they came to. I had never let myself be ensnared by such a desire. It would be ironic indeed, I thought, if at this late age I seemed to be ambushed by it. I comforted myself with the thought that the need was momentary. I was a man of seventy, and not to be carried away by fleeting desires. I also reflected that Sadanand would not stay for long anyway. Once he had left, I would resume my placid life. It is all right to feel a need, and then to try to satisfy it, but often you simply drift into somebody's company, and *then* the need arises. A man must be wary of such insidious perils. But there was little chance that this would happen to me now.

I could not, however, conceal the fact that at the moment Sadanand's presence gave me pleasure. Moreover, I was agitated by recollections of the past. I was not at ease in this state of mind, and therefore suggested to Sadanand that we play a game of *bhendi*. We used to particularly enjoy this game; we played it with place names, though it can be played with other kinds of names. If I said *Ahmedabad,* Sadanand had to pick the final consonant and say, for instance, *Daulatabad.* Then I would come up with something like

Dakar, and Sadanand might surprise me with *Rio de Janeiro,* and so on. In this way scores of places are joined together, however distant from one another they might be. It is like weaving a net, based simply on the fact that the first consonant of a name is identical with the final consonant of another. What is more, the net is woven by an alliance of two minds. It is as if the two coalesce; they do not collide, as in chess.

Slowly we warmed to the game. At first I could not think quickly of appropriate place names, but then I began to toss them off rapidly. At one point Sadanand had to rack his brains for a long time.

While Sadanand was thinking, I realized that I had to make another trip to the lavatory. I told him to take his time, and went to the lavatory assuring myself that, this time, I would surely be successful. Self-confidence is of great importance in life.

The trick paid dividends. Not to repeat the negligence of the morning, I quickly peered down into the basin. The stool was not of normal consistency and color. It looked soft, and pale yellow. But the feeling that my stomach had cleansed itself gave me a sense of relief. By the time I returned, Sadanand had found a place name, which he announced triumphantly.

Soon we tired of the game. As the net of names spreads wider, one begins to wonder if one will ever catch anything in it. Also, what difference does it make if I say *Ahmedabad* and the other person says *Daulatabad,* or the other way round?

Then my stomach started to rumble mildly, and we abandoned the game. For a few minutes the two of us watched the road repairers at work below. Gravel was being mixed with asphalt, laborers shouted, and the steamroller boomed like the beating of a demon's heart. It is in this manner that they make the roads we saunter over.

I was constrained to make yet another visit to the lavatory. This time I found that the lizard had reappeared on the wall. On this occasion I successfully tossed it into the basin, and sent it down the drain. My performance elated me.

The stool resembled the earlier one.

Sadanand inquired if my stomach was disturbed. He said he had some pills with him, but I declined firmly. I avoid medicines, as far as possible. I affected an unperturbed expression to mask my discomfort, but Sadanand seemed aware of it. He thought up something to entertain me. He took down the parrot's cage, asked me to make the parrot talk, and switched on his recorder. "History is on our side," the parrot shrieked. Then Sadanand kept the parrot's cage in front of the mirror and played the tape. "History is on our side," the recorder announced. The parrot in the cage was tricked by the sight of his own reflection in the mirror, and the sound from the recorder. He thought that there was another parrot in front of him. He shrieked, and beat his wings, and lunged against the bars frantically.

The parrot's exertions made Sadanand laugh. He played the tape again, and the parrot fought against the bars more desperately. Sadanand howled with laughter. I watched. Simply because of Sadanand's merriment, there may have been a smile on my face. But in reality I was apprehensive. For one thing, the growing pain in my belly was driving me to distraction. Secondly, I felt that there was something wrong with playing such a prank on the parrot. Whose side is history on, I asked myself, watching the parrot in the cage, and the mirrored parrot in the mirrored cage.

The parrot's struggle made me uneasy. Until now my parrot had lived peacefully. Only once, when a flock of wild parrots passed above the house shrieking, the parrot in the cage listened tensely, and sat motionless for a long while. Otherwise, he was a cheerful companion. And now, observing a parrot in the mirror, he was driven to desperation. With my face contorted by pain, I alternately looked at the parrot in the cage, his reflection in the mirror, and at Sadanand. Outside, the steamroller rumbled, crushing gravel to dust.

The parrot's struggle against the bars had rumpled his feathers, and his eyes were dilated. After some time he looked exhausted. His movements slowed, and his shrieking became shrill. But he continued to struggle fitfully, until he could hardly move. Then suddenly he screamed, "History is on our side," and, with a convulsive movement of his legs, dropped to the floor of the cage. He made no further movement or sound. For a few moments, Sadanand did not realize what had happened. He wiped his eyes, which were watering with laughter, and continued to laugh. Then he noticed the parrot's condition. He froze, and stared at the cage. Then he stood up, and looked alternately at the cage and the mirror.

Sadanand walked towards the cage, and stood in front of it for a few seconds. He opened the door to the cage, and watched intently, as if he expected the parrot to fly out at any moment.

Gingerly Sadanand inserted his hand into the cage, and prodded the parrot with his forefinger. The parrot rolled over, legs in the air. Sadanand reached in further, and clutched the body. He took it out, opened his hand, and stared at the dead parrot. Then, as if something had stung him, he flung the parrot's body into the cage, and quickly shut the door. He turned and looked at me. In his eyes I could read fear and contrition.

I was shaking with each stab of pain in my belly. To make matters worse, my parrot was dead, thanks to the prank played by Sadanand. The parrot that had kept me company for many years was gone, and as for Sadanand he would leave in a day or two.

Was it so hard to do without my parrot?

Perhaps it would have been better if I had not kept a parrot.

If I had not kept a parrot—if Sadanand had not visited me—my mind whirled. Suddenly I was filled with rage against Sadanand. He had killed my parrot. He had made me eat candy, and caused me misery. Perhaps he had put something in the candy? Maybe some kind of poison? Did he come all the way merely to congratulate me on my birthday? No, he had planned to do away with me. He was envious of my book, of the scholarly and dedicated life I had led. He had deceived me by flattery.

My face, twisted with pain, became even more crooked. In a voice that surprised me by its hoarseness, I commanded Sadanand to sit in front of the mirror. Sadanand obeyed, and I switched on his recorder. "Speak," I said.

Sadanand spoke: "The solitary one wears his shoes out. The other takes one by surprise at the end, one day or another, a gun in his hand. Whose steps are imprinted backwards?"

I rewound the tape. "Look into the mirror," I told Sadanand, and played the tape. Sadanand stared at his reflection, and listened to his own words. I rewound the tape, and played it again. Then yet again.

I watched Sadanand. He didn't struggle like the parrot. Motionless, he looked wide-eyed into the mirror, with beads of sweat forming on his forehead. After a few minutes, his whole body began to perspire. Then, very slowly, he rose and walked backwards with measured steps, like a somnambulist. I thought he was going to stumble against the wall behind him. But just as he reached the wall, his legs gave way, and he collapsed to the floor. For a few moments his fingers twitched, as if they were trying to catch hold of something. Then he lay still. I sat looking at Sadanand's body. Then I rose and rushed to the lavatory. When I returned, I felt very weak. My stomach continued to churn. My head swam.

I approached Sadanand's body and, bending down, touched his forehead. Cold as marble. I lifted his hand, and groped for the pulse. There was none. I let go of his hand, and it dropped to the floor. For a moment I stood beside his body, then I turned and went to the window. It was evening, and becoming dark. The workers had gone home. Like a slumbering demon, the steamroller lay by the roadside.

Sunk in my reclining chair, I watched Sadanand's body. There was no sign of the pain in my stomach decreasing. I got up, and took from the cupboard the bottle filled with a powder Jambhekar Shastri had given me many years ago. I swallowed a spoonful of the powder in water, and lay down in bed. Then I had to visit the lavatory again; stumbling out of the bed, I made it to the basin just in time. A few moments' delay, and my loincloth would have been soiled. The stool was thin as water. I sat on, in case my bowels had more to discharge. I wanted my stomach to be purged thoroughly once and for all, and had no inclination to keep repeating my visits to the lavatory.

Squatting over the basin, I discovered that, for no particular reason, I was thinking about the lizard I had disposed of earlier. I was trying to imagine how a lizard died in the water gushing into the basin. Does a lizard really die, I asked myself. In the whirlpool of my mind, the question fluttered without answer. Then I had a strange feeling. In the multitude of thoughts, emotions, and sensations raging in my mind and body, I did not at first clearly apprehend the nature of this feeling. But it grew, and then I realized that it felt like a lizard, which had emerged from the lavatory basin, was entering my rectum. I did my best to suppress this feeling, and endeavored to convince myself that such a thing was inconceivable. My attempt was fruitless. More and more powerfully I had the sensation of a lizard squirming its way up my rectum.

Giddily I came out of the lavatory, and threw myself into bed. I stared at the ceiling. Then I sat up and, moving with difficulty, walked towards Sadanand's body. I stooped, and attempted to lift it, but to no avail. Somehow I dragged him to the bed, and hauled him up. I rolled him over to the other side of the bed, close to the wall. I puffed heavily. I had exerted myself knowing full well that, in my condition, it was not wise to do so. Probably owing to the strain of this activity, I had a fresh urge to relieve myself. I scarcely had the strength to go and squat upon the basin, but, telling myself that this would be the last time, I made it to the lavatory.

Nothing came. I continued to sit uselessly. And then, as I had half expected, the sensation I had felt earlier rose again. I had killed countless lizards in this lavatory. You could say I had become addicted to these little occasions for excitement. And now all those lizards were clambering up the basin, and jostling to invade me. My whole body shook.

After a while it became impossible to remain squatting. It appeared equally difficult to stand up, but, supporting myself against the wall, I managed it. I staggered into the bedroom, and collapsed in bed. The sensation of lizards slithering up my rectum one after the other became unbearably acute. I thrashed my legs upon the bed.

I thought that I should not have done what I did to Sadanand. If he were alive now, he would have helped me. Sadanand was a nice man. He would have helped me, and taken care of me. And what terrible thoughts I had entertained in my mind regarding him! He played with the parrot only to amuse me. He had come from so far away to congratulate me, and I had suspected his intentions. Now all that remained of him was the cold body beside me. With my mind in tumult, I stretched out my arm, and touched Sadanand's face. Gently I moved my hand over his face, and over his chest. I let it rest on his chest. I could scarcely stand the feeling of creatures squeezing in between my legs, but I clamped my thighs together.

Late in the night I thought I heard the sound of rain. Then there was the peculiar smell of the first monsoon rains falling upon the dusty ground. Things were already beginning to assume their daylight shapes when I fell asleep.

BY THE CLEMENCY OF HELL/
SKETCHES FOR PURGATORY

MONTRI UMAVIJANI

BY THE CLEMENCY OF HELL

For M.M.N.G.

AUTHOR'S NOTE: *Hell is a time-consciousness. Other aspects of time, such as past, present, and future, reveal themselves as distinct from each other and subject to change and obliteration. Hell is, essentially, those moments made wholly present to the conscious mind. Legends often say that some people go to hell after death. That can only be true insofar as a certain supernatural power could metamorphose the dead into pure consciousnesses. The poet, on the other hand, is by nature capable of experiencing hell in living. He minutely encompasses hell. His writings are, however, respites from that preoccupation. Only in the immortality of the work that hell is finally exorcized.*

So many years after the events and the feelings, these pieces of mine are offered to the reader. They form one poem which has come into being by the clemency of hell.—M.U., Bangkok 1977

1/ INVOCATION TO HELL

What do I owe it for having been there?
Surely, hell's time cannot with time be
unwound:

my life as having not lived;
my death as having not died.

2/ HELL

I have often succumbed—
and brought down temptation
with my unyielding clutch;
I have touched all depths and rebounded
sky high to other
darknesses.

3/ A PLIGHT

Sometime,
she will have to run after life,
or do something heartbreakingly
simple.

4/ HELL

One cannot be in hell for nothing,
as from nothing
nothing can be;
hell is where
nothing looks at nothing:
hell—not seeing.

5

For her I am a thing for thought,
perhaps for tears when they come;
had my heart burst,
she would have grieved enough
for the event, which,

to her best knowledge, would be
as eventual as it is
inevitable.

6

Out of this hell
may my going be
abysmal.

7

One does not go from hell
as bird from a cage:
a hell-flight takes to
an infernal altitude
amidst a burning firmament.

8/ PRAYER

Have pity on me, O Lord,
I am depressed and—
worse than dead.

9/ A VISIT

Perhaps I have been to see the dead,
the dead whose kindly smile
gleams in my cadaverous hope—
my dearest hope of despair!

10

Long hours I wait, always I wait:
hell is waiting with me
till the waiting is over.

11/ A TELEPHONE CONVERSATION

Listen to me well:
if now I go from you,
not a thousand other worlds
will contain me.

12/ DESPAIR

My anonymous sorrow:
that afternoon, anyone
could have walked up to her
and spent as much cavernous time
to come wind-blown to this pass.

13/ HELL

That night hell was rampant:
I could say nothing
to make her believe;
my vision was all dark,
while my heart was burning.

14/ PARIS

After so much pain,
I brought to a close
my baggage and my stay.

15

I have seen tears flow fast—
in hell it did not matter.

16/ HELL

It is true that hell has
by lassive clemency
distended me;
but I am sent out for nothing,
and where I meet nothing,
I wander still
in hell's immensity.

17/ IN PASSAGE

I heard, in passage,
my condemnation
spoken clearly in the voice
of the exterminating angel,
and I looked for her, my love,
my love in hell,
even where she was pressed
in her solitude:
my fiery hope
once again leapt to
its impasse.

18/ DESTINY

Perhaps the superseding worm
for once will be kind
when I break life open
to meet with him.

19/ THE WOMAN

Nothing's left of that long time:
she has lived through it,
while I, my Lord, have only begun
to relive.

may the hyacinths
not smell after fading.

30

Already I have thought:
hell's clemency
has given me
those years in my hands,
glittering and
infinitesimal.

31/ THE GIRL

She waits without saying,
she thinks when nothing else;
when I am gone,
oh may not the Lord
pluck me
from my thoughtful receding.

32/ LIFE

We live
between an extreme
weariness and an extreme
passion—
woe to him in whom
these two meet.

33

It seems like
she had piled between us
unreal things:
years, husband, children;

but when I look at her,
weary with those,
my passion for once became
unreal.

34

Thus said I to my fate:
"This, sir, is not the way
to punish me;
I have known all the pains,
had hell-fires burned my veins,
yet I have been told
my perdition is not immediate."

35/ THE WOMAN

I am but a memory to her;
with all my being
I could not make real
my once most weary
passion.

36

I must go there,
my heart within me burns:
yes, hell has let me loose
for more losses.

37/ ROME

I put together my wits
and place them
before a chance.

38/ LAST CHANCE

My last chance
is thrown up against the sky
to break into starry
futilities.

39/ LIFE

Life has taken
a terrible
vengeance on me;
but I also
have from it
exacted every possible
humor.

40/ CONFRONTATION

My terrible humor
will not wait
for this funereal march,
but will override it
to a greater futility.

41/ A VENGEANCE

A terrible vengeance:
my life, my all-desired,
finds its last stoppage;
my hopes are submerged
in primeval mud.

42/ A NIGHT

In that night were contained
my hopes, my all;

I let it pass—
I, slept in my anguish.

43/ THE CHANCE

It has come to pass:
my discus
has missed the sun
and flown past
many oceans.

44/ A FAULT

A fault as fundamental
as hills and seas;
a fault which aspires and heaves
for eternities.

45/ MY CRY

My cry
has found its harbor
where nothing, pale as a star,
reigns absolute.

46

In the solitude of hell,
memories, regrets piled up
until the heart was full.

47/ HELL

I must live hell
the fullest;

I must
plumb once more
the spectral depths,
and I must hope to emerge
to hope
to find my hope waiting.

48

The qualities of my lived time
are such that if I speak
silence gathers thickly
around my utterance.

SKETCHES FOR PURGATORY

AUTHOR'S NOTE: *Purgatory is a multilayer consciousness. It is chiefly a present negated against the background of its own past and future. It thus becomes a not-now, an indescribable moment which is at once brief and interminable. Religious poets in the West have placed purgatory between hell and paradise. In Buddhist cosmology, however, purgatory is a region of hell called* lokanta *which is, literally, at the boundary of the worlds. This region can be shown by putting together three circles.*

The writing program which I attended at an American university seemed to have induced in me this mood of purgatory. In my earlier volume, hell was a closed world with a moving exit so that the traveler could not get out of it. As for purgatory, it has many exits all of which are stationary. As a result, the consciousness keeps darting off into different worlds, only to come back to the present in such pieces as are entitled "Writing," etc.

This is my second attempt in the musical mode.—M. U., Bangkok 1979.

IOWA CITY & CHICAGO

1/ INVOCATION TO HELL

Even out there,
my mantric name
stuck to me
with an umbilical cord:
the nameless creatures,
venomous and hateful,
hung back at each call,
unable to sneer at
the fate in the name.

2/ WHAT A MOTHER SAID TO HER CHILD

The rolley coach takes you up in the air—
scream and howl whatever you want—
until it stops.

3/ PURGATORY

Press closely three circles,
and see the space between them:
there lie
the past that is not,
the present that cannot be,
and the future that will not be.

4/ A PAST

I will have to unlearn
how I have come out of hell
enough
to call it a time.

5/ THE CROWD AT THE POMPEII EXHIBIT

These people are here
to see their past lives,
unremembered and, therefore,
endurable.

6/ WRITING

My three fingers
drive the pen outward;
the axis moves
from my hand

to my shoulder,
then, to my throat,
reaching up to my head,
and going out in smoke.

7/ HER VOICE ON THE PHONE

Furtive in its familiarity,
her voice rang and eluded.

8/ A YOUNG POET

Waiting on the front row,
he looks
something between celebrity and
celibacy,
not knowing how to choose
between the schoolgirl love
and the old hag fame.

9/ A GIRL

The distance—
after the beer, the talks,
and the mushroom
with a faded love—
how shall I call this?

10/ THE COUPLE

Having lived together awhile,
they have one mind, even
their rear ends look alike,
subject
to the same confinement
and the same locomotion.

11/ A PLIGHT

I reach out to many,
so I can reach out to one;
what I have failed with many
will be regained in the one.

12/ POMPEII

I have longed to tell her:
you are a Pompeiian;
that soft curve of you, I remember,
was silhouetted against the wall,
one pair of hands groped for it,
then another, and yet another,
making the shadow indistinct—
that night the warm flood came on us.

13/ PENANCE

My stomach has curved in:
wine has the taste of ashes,
and I look at women
as just skeletons holding
empty cups.

14/ THE NIGHT IN CANTERBURY

I remember the joy:
my words became language
when they had
a hearing.

15/ SITUATION

Sitting between a flower
and a flower,

life threatened to become
a tree, reaching out,
roots and branches,
vertically.

16/ A CHOICE

I've chosen my life—
the dejection and the isolation—
because from such a narrow path
I may reach out.

17/ TOMORROW

Tomorrow will come
with an ache of getting up,
looking out of the window,
getting out in the cold air,
going, always going,
and getting nowhere.

18/ APPROACHING WINTER

The fingers of cold
feel for my face,
stroke my hair and
brush across my forehead,
but just miss my eyes.

19/ FROM THE AIRPORT

On the glassy road,
going
at a high speed,
I contemplate my death:

not the death that must come,
but the death that could come
a little too soon.

20/ THE DEATH OF A FEELING

Just smothered
by the first air it took:
I saw the eyes upturned,
sweet upon another's eyes.

21/ WAITING

It is snowing outside,
inside it must be warm;
I knock at the door
and plead,
hoping that her heart
will thaw out.

22/ TALK

Snow descended
and wrapped me around;
I tried to speak up,
but could only make a
monologue.

23

Time was,
we played a tender and
obdurate game:
my reach often
overreached itself,

and your indifference
sometimes
made a difference.

24/ A STORE GOING OUT OF BUSINESS

I was there often before,
now I go in among ghouls,
not to grab things for myself,
but to help it go
with dignity.

25/ THE CLOTHING STORE

It's gone,
like a fabric torn
between a past and a future;
in that explosion of lint,
I threw in
my thread and needle.

26/ WRITING

I only know writing
as a falling away from,
and a getting close to,
but what it is
I am not given to know.

27/ WRITING

I sit before a work,
like a man who has
no past and no future,
poised at the moment of fusion,

when the mind penetrates into
nothingness.

28/ PREDICAMENT

Like a prophet
who has nothing to proclaim,
I sit in an alley way,
observing quietly,
with my back turned
to the company
of those who sit up against mountains,
and those who stand up against walls.

29/ PURGATORY

Purgatory
is hell halved
into things
diametrically opposed,
which come together,
such as
dinner for one and
double occupancy.

30/ PURGATORY

The exit no longer
moves before me:
I push and pass through;
O Lord, this is not hell,
as you promised,
but how many exits
I will have to make,
and what knowledge
I will come out with?

31/ A CHILD SAID TO ANOTHER CHILD

I am here,
I sit by the window,
the window is here:
I am here.

HONOLULU & TOKYO

32

I will go and see
what damnation has to say
about my life.

33/ DEPARTURE

Between something that will not come
and something that does not come,
I set again
my route.

34/ WRITING

Even such as I
am sometimes given
fecund moments
in which to dot paper
endlessly
with my pointillist pen.

35/ A THOUGHT

As I grow older,
my years run together

and go down the crack
you once opened in my heart,
unintentionally.

36/ MOMENT

Light fell on us—
a discreet light,
making its paved way
through the chill and dusty air,
as I was reading your love.

37/ ON A PICTURE POSTCARD

My feeling for you
is like a flower blooming
in an empty room.

38/ A MEAL ON THE PLANE

The taste
of that noodle
reminded me
of the tomb
where we lay together
in Nagazagi.

39/ THE WOMAN

I wanted to cry out to her:
"We died together, once,
and lay side by side."
But now,
as before,

I despaired
of reaching for her.

40

The fault was not hers at all:
she was not given the insight,
while I had too much of it
to relate to her well
in the present.

41/ THE WOMAN

A few words from her
rang across
the space of forgetfulness,
such words as:
"I have no doubt about it,"
speaking of our future
encounter,
from a distant past.

42

The taste of the noodle
is the cold tomb where we lay
in Nagazagi.

43/ A PAST

After the fall,
I tried
again and again,
intent on any sign
of recognition.

44/ LOVE

I look from one face
to another;
now I know:
love is a manner of
particularizing.

45/ LOVE

No one
can claim to love,
for love is
a general attitude
which yet
particularizes.

46/ PERCEPTION

My particularizing eyes
caught this rainy evening
a girl carrying an umbrella,
and followed her
until they found
no girl, no umbrella,
only evening
and rain.

47

Divinity must be
particularizing without
particularizing.

48/ EXPECTATION

My expectation
climbs the stone steps

to reach a temple
of austere
isolation.

49/ THE EVENING

After this time,
I will never see her again;
I now depart
with her correct address.

50

Already I have tried,
and no response,
I cease in awe,
for to go on in that way,
I would trespass
the domain of my Lord.

50/ THE OLD FRIEND

I told her:
the little I gain
from knowing people
will increase
and freeze into
a divinity.

52/ TOKYO

I must call on
the lives I have lived there
for the final chance to walk on it,
measuring my grave.

FABLE OF THE SO-CALLED BIRDS

A Picaresque Imbecility

LAWRENCE FERLINGHETTI

Hommage à Jacques Prévert

In Rome
a woman goes to the powder room
and puts on another face
When she comes out
her husband does not know her
and takes her for a famous movie director
and takes her to the top
of the town of Spoleto
where they rent a room in an aviary
and proceed to take off
each other's feathers
And he's a red bird and she's a blue bird
but without their feathers they look alike
When they have finished
they take their feathers
and put them together in a big pillow
which they sleep on together
and in the morning
try to separate their feathers
Then they walk out into the Piazza dei Duomo

where they are immediately captured naked
by the town birdcatcher
who runs with them to the Prince of the town
claiming they are twin love birds
from the Garden of Eden
who had to paste on feathers
so they wouldn't be taken
for Adam & Eve
But they are taken only for naked birds
who shouldn't be wandering around
without their feathers
and the polizia start chasing them
all over Italia
since it is obviously against the law
of gravity
for birds to go around without feathers
And so they run all over Umbria
with the polizia chasing them
with bags of feathers and pots of glue
And St. Francis has no sight of them
as they run past Assisi
but this is a fable
and Umbria a Communist district
and so when all the other wild animals
see what is happening to the two naked birds
with the polizia pursuing them
they call a Congress of Birds in Perugia
and vote to form a Union of Unfeathered Birds
and some red geese from Castiglione del Lago
offer their own lakeside nests
to the two naked birds
And so they settle down there
in the Commune di Castiglione del Lago
And Christ who was hung up crucified
in the local church on the main street
just as He is hung up
in every church around the world
comes down to the lake
and throws the nails from his hands

into the lake
and strokes the two birds with his bleeding hands
And His hands are healed
and He says Thank You and walks away over a hill
carrying His cross again
as if nothing had ever happened
but the two naked birds fish His nails
out of the lake and take them
to the Union of Shoemakers in town
and the shoemakers are so grateful
for these magic nails
that they give the two birds jobs as apprentices
And in this little shoe shop
the master cobbler has a pair of blackbirds
who he has trained to pick up nails
and bring them to him one at a time
as he needs them
but while they are bringing the nails
they begin whispering in the ears
of the two naked birds
whispering to them that they too
had once been free birds
but that now they were enslaved
just like workers everywhere
because now that they had shoes
they wanted socks
and when they got socks
they wanted pants and shirts
and when they had them
they wanted coats and hats and brassières
and nylons and neckties and houses and jewelry
and fur coats and sports cars
and everything they wanted they
would have to pay for
they would have to work for
and it was obviously a capitalist plot
to enslave all workers everywhere
And the two crows paint such a horrible picture
of the capitalist consumer world

that the two naked birds
throw off their new shoes
and run over the horizon to Siena
where they run into a very strange bird indeed
who claims he can make feathers grow again
all over them
if they would only join
the Mystic Feather & Hairgrowers Union
but at this very moment in Siena
in the great shell-shaped Piazza
the natives are running the big horse race
the Palio
in which all the neighborhoods of Siena
compete with each other
and each district has one horse
and they each have their banner and their colors
and they race around the stone Piazza
at breakneck speeds waving their banners
And now the district called Owl
the Civetta
wins the race
because the mascot owl
is riding on the head of the horse
and telling it how to run wisely
And when the naked birds
see the wise owl winning
with all its feathers on
and the prize wreath around its neck
they go running up to the owl
and ask him
how he remains so free and swift
and yet manages to retain all his feathers
And the Owl nods his head without answering
and in the process of nodding his head
falls sound asleep
And in his sleep he hears himself hooting
And they hear him hooting that night
when they are sleeping
And it is a bad sign

the sound of him at night is a bad sign
a sign that something bad
is going to happen to you
And so the next day they get up very early
and run away again
to San Gimignano
the town of many towers on a high hill
over a valley of vineyards
And they run through the valley at sunset
and reach San Gimignano
just as the swallows and pigeons
rise up to the tops of the trees & towers
to sing to the setting sun
And they too try to fly
to the tops of the towers
which were built by powerful families
each trying to prove
it was greater than the other
by building higher than the other
And the two naked birds realize
they cannot ever fly high enough
unless they grow real feathers again
and accept their natural condition again
but this they cannot do
because once the feathers are plucked
they do not grow back like hair
and it is like losing their virginity
in the Garden of Eden
and they can never fly purely and simply again
And so they give it all up
and crawl back to Rome in the night
And take up Science
and learn aerodynamics and invent rocketry
and migrate to the United States of America
and give up Communism
and join the Space program
and shoot off in a rocket to the moon
and fall back to earth
and try always to fly

to still higher and higher places
but always fall back to earth with parachutes
And as they fall they hear
way below and far away
the so-various singing of small free birds
hidden in green hills
in a garden called Love
in a district no longer shown on maps
and no longer represented
in the national legislature.

FIVE POEMS

EDWIN BROCK

THE NATURE OF MEMORY

On a day which
might as well be Monday
in a small house in a poor street
a dog which
might as well be our mongrel
went mad in the kitchen.
Drooling white froth mixed with blood
from the lip it had torn on a nail
it yelped in circles and jumped
as high as a man up the kitchen wall.
I was five and
I was not afraid until
the woman who might as well be my mother
screamed It's mad, it's mad and ran
from the room slamming the door
loud and finally behind her.

This is memory: it is winter and
the afternoon light is fading outside.
I am in a room and

a dog is trying to jump the wall.
It is stupid after half a century
to pretend I can remember
anything of fear. But perhaps just as
stupid to pretend there was nothing.
Today there are simply facts to recall:
>   1. The dog had drunk disinfectant
>   and was burning inside.
>   2. My father came home and drowned him
>   in the stone copper.
>   3. My mother joked about
>   shutting the dog and me together.
>   4. I was five. That is all.

Fifty years is almost a period of history:
The man who drowned the dog is
dead but his wife is still alive.
There have been children, grandchildren
and one great-grandchild. Letters
have come through the post. There
have been floods, droughts and
even a war. It is stupid to pretend
I can remember anything of fear,
equally stupid to say there was nothing.
Let us call the day Monday,
let us note that it happened,
let us regret the feeling that has
drained from everything but remember
that it was the dog who died.

DRY AUTUMN

These are the curling years
we fill with comment:
the weather slopes downhill,
our daughter grows
and goes away.

I have the feeling
our life settles in you
like hourglass sand
and that your hips broaden
benevolently to take it.

Today lightens slowly;
behind a country mist
our doors are closed;
I am waiting for one last leaf
to fall from that alder

before this confession
turns over into dream.

THE SPINE OF THE MALVERNS

Hardly mountaineering:
Saturday families jump across it,
three generations and a dog; the cafe owner
makes its point in a family Ford;
we sip his tea, eat beans on toast,
people of the plains. And yet
the Midland winds lean on Wales
and we have fourteen counties in our pocket
to spend on change. It is not enough:
we know the shrunken world's a visual trick
which grows towards us
and that around any bend
we could meet two people walking,
the size of despair.

FEVER

A gas-mantle turned too low
sucks in its own shadows
and then, out of darkness,
pushes them to the walls.

Thus anything behind, say,
a marble washstand may
reach forward to almost
the sheet of the hot bed.

Screams are no use at all:
she will lie down in your sweat
and stifle you with the heat
of one enormous thigh.

IN THE BLITZ

It was after a tea of
wartime bread and jam
among utility china and
the week's ration of marge:
she looked at my hand and
in the way of someone who
sees through windows said
"Yes, you are going to be
very clever." She was a
warm blonde pretty woman
in a fur coat, and I
would have taken her seriously
except I think my step-
father was fucking her.

NOTES ON CONTRIBUTORS

WALTER ABISH was born in Vienna, spent part of his childhood in Shanghai, and lived for several years in Israel, where he studied urban planning and served in the Israeli army, before settling in the United States in the early 1950s. His fiction and poetry have appeared in various periodicals, including *The Paris Review, Partisan Review, Triquarterly,* and *New American Review.* New Directions has published his novel *Alphabetical Africa* (1974) and his short fiction collections *Minds Meet* (1975) and *In the Future Perfect* (1977). Mr. Abish was awarded a National Endowment for the Arts writing fellowship for 1980 and an Ingram Merrill grant for his newest novel, *How German Is It,* on the ND fall 1980 list.

After his discharge at age twenty-one from the Royal Navy's Pacific fleet, EDWIN BROCK returned to the working-class suburb where he was born and worked in London, first as an editorial assistant on a trade paper and later as a metropolitan policeman. Since 1959 he has commuted between his part-time position at a large London advertising agency and the converted Norfolk granary where he lives with his family. He is poetry editor of the English literary magazine *Ambit,* and his poems have appeared in such American magazines as *The New Yorker, Antaeus,* and *Partisan Review.* New Directions has published his satirical *Paroxisms* (1974), an autobiographical work, *Here. Now. Always.* (1977), and four books of his poetry. His most recent collection, *The River and the Train,* came out in 1979.

For information on poets ANNE-MARIE ALBIACH, JEAN DAIVE, EMMANUEL HOCQUARD, CLAUDE ROYET-JOURNOUD, BERNARD NOËL, and ALAIN VEINSTEIN, and translator PAUL BUCK, see the notes following the selection of their work, "Six French Poets."

FREDERICK BUSCH lives in upstate New York, where he teaches English at Colgate University. His critical study on John Hawkes was published in 1973 by Syracuse University Press, and New Directions subsequently published two of his novels, *Manual Labor* (1974) and *Domestic Particulars* (1976). His stories have been included in past ND anthologies as well as in *New American Review* and *Penguin Modern Stories 9*, and last year Alfred A. Knopf brought out a collection entitled *Hardwater Country*. *The Mutual Friend*, a novel about Charles Dickens, was published in 1978 by Harper & Row, and Busch's latest novel, *Rounds*, was released earlier this year by Farrar, Straus & Giroux.

The *Selected Poems* of GUNNAR EKELÖF (1907–1968) were translated from the Swedish by Muriel Rukeyser and Leif Sjöberg and brought out by Irvington Publishers in 1967. Translator MARCELLA MATTHEI was born of a Swedish noble family and has lived in Turkey, Hawaii, France, Mexico, and the Bahamas, and currently makes her home in Santa Barbara. In 1979, ND brought out KENNETH REXROTH's co-translation (with Ling Chung) of the *Complete Poems* of Li Ch'ing-chao as well as a new collection of Rexroth's own poetry, *The Morning Star*.

The American Library Association listed LAWRENCE FERLINGHETTI's *Landscapes of Living & Dying* as one of the best books of 1979. Early next year, New Directions will publish a signed, limited edition of Ferlinghetti's *A Trip to Italy and France*, from which "The Fable of the So-called Birds" is taken.

ALLEN GROSSMAN was born in 1932 in Minneapolis and educated at Harvard. He is a professor of English at Brandeis University and has been awarded the Garrison Prize for poetry and the prize of the Academy of American poets. His third collection, *The Woman on the Bridge Over the Chicago River* (New Directions, 1979) has received wide critical acclaim.

SAMUEL HAZO is the director of The International Poetry Forum at the Carnegie Library in Pittsburgh and a professor of English at Duquesne University. His most recent book of poems, *An American Made in Paris*, was published by the International Poetry Forum in 1978. New Directions will be bringing out *To Paris* in the near future.

Born in 1942 in Schwerte, West Germany, RÜDIGER KREMER studied German literature, art history, and journalism at the universities of Münster and Vienna. From 1968 to 1972 he was an editor at Radio Bremen, and he is now a free-lance writer in that city. The most recent of Kremer's three radio plays, "Second Session on the Color of Snow" (*"Zweite Sitzung über die Farbe des Schnees"*) ran approximately forty-five minutes when it was first produced in Germany in October 1977. BREON MITCHELL, whose translations of Kremer's work have also appeared in *ND27 and ND33*, is associate professor of German and Comparative Literature at Indiana University. His *James Joyce and the German Novel* was published in 1976 by Ohio University Press.

Born in 1914 in southern Chile, NICANOR PARRA has held graduate fellowships at Oxford and Brown universities and is presently professor of theoretical physics at the University of Chile. In 1937, when his first book of poems was published in Santiago, the simple, direct, ironic idiom which he called "antipoetry" was immediately acclaimed as a "new voice" in Spanish-language poetry. In 1971, ND brought out Parra's *Poems and Antipoems,* a bilingual edition with translations by Fernando Alegría, Lawrence Ferlinghetti, Allen Ginsberg, Denise Levertov, Thomas Merton, W. S. Merwin, Miller Williams, and William Carlos Williams. *Emergency Poems,* translated by Miller Williams, was published in 1972. "The Sermons and Preaching of the Christ of Elqui" is translated by EDITH GROSSMAN, who is the author of *The Antipoetry of Nicanor Parra,* published by New York University Press in 1975.

Ever since his first collection of fiction, *Color of Darkness* (New Directions, 1957) won him critical acclaim, JAMES PURDY has been a strong presence on the literary scene. Arbor House has published his most recent novels: *In a Shallow Grave* (1976), *Narrow Rooms* (1978), and *The Mourners Below* (1980).

MARK RUDMAN is co-editor and translator of *Square of Angels: The Selected Poems of Bohdan Antonyich* (Ardis Press, 1977) and *Orchard Lamps: Poems by Ivan Drach* (The Sheep Meadow Press, 1978) and the author of a book on Robert Lowell, forthcoming from Columbia University Press. He is the editor of *Pequod: A Journal of Contemporary Literature and Literary Criticism.*

VILAS SARANG was educated in Bombay and at Indiana University and teaches English at the University of Basra, Iraq. His stories have appeared in *Encounter, The Malahat Review, Mundus Artium, Triquarterly,* and the Penguin anthology *New Writing in India.* He has translated into his native Marathi works by Yeats, Auden, Eliot, and Beckett, and has published a collection of poems, *A Kind of Silence* (Calcutta, 1978). BREON MITCHELL also translated the Rüdiger Kremer radio play included in these pages.

JOHN TAGGART teaches at Shippensburg State College (Pa.). His poetry books are: *To Construct a Clock, The Pyramid is a Pure Crystal, Prism & the Pine Twig,* and most recently *Dodeka.*

A university professor at Ta Prachandra, Bangkok, MONTRI UMAVIJANI writes poetry in both Thai and English and is also a critic of Thai literature. His first book of verse, *The Intermittent Image,* was published in 1968, and he has since published five additional volumes and earned his Ph.D. at Northwestern University.

GABRIEL ZAID was born in Mexico in 1934. He is the author of *Cuestionario: Poems 1951–1976,* published by Fondo de Cultura Economica, and has translated the songs of Vidyapati (1978). He is on the editorial board of *Vuelta.* CARLOS ALTSCHUL, along with Monique Altschul, has translated Ernesto Cardenal's *Homage to American Indians* (Johns Hopkins Press, 1973). MARGARET RANDALL is an American expatriot who first settled in Mexico, where for eight years she co-published the influential literary magazine *El Corno Emplumado.* After the 1968 student massacre in Mexico City, she fled to Havana, where she now works at the Social Sciences Publishing House of the Cuban Book Institute. Her political autobiography, *Part of the Solution,* was published by New Directions in 1973. ELIOT WEINBERGER, who lives in New York City, is the publisher and editor of the literary magazine *Montemora* and the translator of two collections by Octavio Paz *Eagle or Sun?* (1976) and *A Draft of Shadows and Other Poems* (1980), both published by New Directions.